Having received great interest and positive feedback from the readers of her first two books, *Relatively Distant* and *Neighbourhood Watch*, Gemma was encouraged by the appetite of her readers for a third book. With this in mind, she embarked on the final instalment of what she now refers to as '*The Emma Series*'. As with the two previous books, *Staying Relevant* is the final book of a trilogy, but is also a standalone book, with its own story to tell. Again, her home county is all the inspiration needed for the location of *Staying Relevant*. Waterport resonates with most people that live in a close-knit community, that sometimes feels like everybody knows each other.

Gemma Bolger

To my readers—past, present and future.

Gemma Bolger

STAYING RELEVANT

AUSTIN MACAULEY PUBLISHERS™

LONDON • CAMBRIDGE • NEW YORK • SHARJAH

A CIP catalogue record for this title is available from the British Library.

ISBN 9781035833795 (Paperback)
ISBN 9781035833801 (ePub e-book)

www.austinmacauley.co.uk

First Published 2024
Austin Macauley Publishers Ltd®
1 Canada Square
Canary Wharf
London
E14 5AA

Once again, I'd like to acknowledge and thank my husband, Pat, and our sons, Patrick, Joseph, Seán and Darragh, for supporting me and encouraging me to write *Staying Relevant*. To all those who have taken the time to read *Relatively Distant* and *Neighbourhood Watch*, know that it is much appreciated, and I extend my thanks. As always, I would like to acknowledge the friendly professionalism and efficiency of the Austin Macauley team.

Closer to home, thanks to the big cohort of readers in Waterford, who usually frequent 'The Book Centre' and to the very pleasant staff therein, who always remind me to come in and sign some copies!

Prologue
Early Autumn 2020

We're all in this together.

"Did you ever feel like you should have done things differently?"

Matty is sitting on a park bench and airs this question to his silent but attentive companion. Not waiting for an answer Matty sighs deeply and feels bitterly let down. "We'll lock down for a few weeks, they said, and then you'll get your lives back." A couple of passers-by glance at the old man on the bench talking to himself with the little white dog at his feet, but Matty doesn't even notice. More than ever, Matty feels that his life choices were a mistake. Before the pandemic, it didn't bother him that he had never married and had lived most of his life alone, but now he feels he's worlds apart from those who had settled down to marriage and had children. Feeling now his friend Bobby has abandoned him, they had tried Zoom calls in the early days of lockdown, but neither of them were great with technology and their conversations had been stilted and awkward. They had promised themselves they would go for a pint in Ryan's Bar as soon as things had got back to normal and that had turned out to be a longer wait than either of them thought possible.

When things did finally open up and they could have a pint once they bought a nine-euro meal—they ended up sitting outside under a canopy that was leaking rain in on them and gave up and went home after half an hour. Matty hasn't seen Bobby since and their only contact has been by phone. Matty knows that Bobby is in a better place for dealing with a pandemic than he is, as Bobby is surrounded by family and has his wife living with him and adult children dropping by with shopping most days.

Getting ready to tread his weary way home, Matty begins to button his coat up. Just as he is about to stand, a well-dressed man in his early fifties sits on the other end of the bench and with a smile, strikes up a conversation with Matty. Ignoring his instincts and the growl coming from under the bench, Matty is glad of the company and settles back down to enjoy a long chat with this friendly, familiar looking man. Paul Lombard is not wearing a mask and Matty soon recognises him.

If the world wasn't such a stark and lonely place for Matty, he may have made his excuses and left. But the world is a very different place now and Matty is in desperate need of the company. Paul however doesn't recognise Matty, as Matty is wearing a face mask. There is a watery cold sun today and Matty's eyes tend to water when they are exposed to it, so he's also wearing his sunglasses. As Paul is doing most of the talking, he doesn't get to hear much of Matty's voice either, just the odd mumble of agreement as Paul offloads—he is lonely too.

When Matty does eventually get home, a couple of hours have passed. Glad now that he had stayed, he feels much better about his lot. Marvelling at how simple human contact can lift the spirit—Matty decides not to tell Bobby about his new friend. He knows Bobby wouldn't approve and as his late mother would have said, beggars can't be choosers.

Chapter 1
October 2021
Stay Connected

The half-light of dawn creeps across the city below. From Paul's vantage point high above the city, he knew among the now diminishing orange city lights that his tormentor was starting to stir awake. In his uniform pocket he can feel the envelope and is reminded with a shiver of the message that lies within. Knowing that the sender could ruin his life in a more permanent way than he has managed himself, leaves him cold. Arriving with the rest of the post at home that morning, Paul is relieved that he had gotten hold of the post before his wife had. Coming in from his shift, he had met the postman just as he was about to make his delivery.

At first he was intrigued by the lilac coloured envelope that had a familiar perfume to it, his name and address were written so neatly that it took him only a couple of seconds to realise that a stencil must have been used. The message inside had simply said, "Missing you, hope to see you soon, love Penny." To someone else, the content would seem harmless enough, the lettering was made up of cut up newspapers and there was a small sketch of a mermaid in the far right hand corner of the page. Added to this was the fact that Penny was dead and he was the one that had rolled her into the sea many years ago made him very nervous.

Paul is standing in what was once the busiest dancefloor in the Waterport area and had attended many functions and parties there himself in his younger life. The Ardview Hotel played host to most big social occasions up to the late nineties, including his own wedding. There were panoramic views of the whole city from the vast floor to ceiling windows that took in the quayside and the sprawling city right out to the green tinged edges of suburbia and beyond. These views were the backdrop to most of his and Clara's wedding photographs and for many other local couples also. Perched high on the clifftop and only separated by a river from the main shopping area of Waterport, the Ardview was once a much sought after and popular venue for the social scene of Waterport. The local newspapers would be full every week with pictures of people attending the various gatherings that were held there. Now it lay in tatters.

As he makes his way through the ground floor, he has to step over pieces of the large white ceiling tiles that are scattered throughout the hotel. Electrical wires are dangling over his head and at some points he has to dip his head so as not to touch them. The only light source left now is the emergency lighting. Bizarrely the large disco ball that is centred in the ceiling still picks up the greenish glow from the exit signs.

Paul doesn't like to dwell in this particular part of the ground floor, too many ghosts. It's hard to imagine but beneath the debris and discarded bottles and beer cans the large expansive hardwood dancefloor has remained intact.

The very same floorboards that he and Clara had their first dance at their wedding on. Not quite believing how much has changed since then, so many gone now that had been filmed laughing and dancing on their wedding video between these four walls. With an overwhelming sense of loss, he gives a heavy sigh and continues on his rounds.

Passing by the now drained swimming pool, he imagines he hears a scuttling noise from its now dry floor. Running the beam of his flashlight over the pool area, he catches what he perceives to be a rat's tail disappearing under a pile of leaves that have blown in through the missing panels in the glazed dome ceiling above. Relief mixes with disgust and he picks up his pace.

Consoling himself he only had a couple of hours left on his shift, he was heartened by the light starting to fill the sky and finishes his last round of walking the ground floor before he heads back to the reception area and the unfinished crossword that he has been dragging out for the night. His fellow security guard, Tommy, is fast asleep in the small office that is directly behind the large wood panelled reception desk. Both Paul and Tommy are ex-garda and have come to an arrangement with regards to getting through the long twelve hour night shift. They take turns sleeping. Pulling two of the best redundant mattress from one of the upstairs hotel rooms, they split the night between them. Being careful to bring their sleeping bags and pillows home with them every morning to avoid being caught out with their little arrangement, it works well for both of them and shortens the night.

Draining the last of his coffee from the flask, he settles down to finally fill in the last four letters on his crossword.

The clue offered: profoundly immoral and wicked, beginning with E. Knowing his answer to be wrong but so right also, Paul grins. With jerky stabbing motions, Paul scrawls deliberately and slowly—EMMA.

Paul is not the only one regretting serious mistakes from the past, Judge Ciara Donnelly is glad to get up as she has had another restless night. Incredulous that only a short six months has passed since all was well in her world. Constantly hearing about how bad things are because of the pandemic, she is having her own personal crisis as well. Doubting her sanity when she thinks about her recent dubious and definitely illegal activities that Paul has driven her to. It had seemed harmless enough when she started to flirt with the then Detective Lombard. Now she sees with full clarity that she should have run a mile when he first asked her to 'bend the rules'.

Usually, weak women that were manipulated by men disgusted her—she now knows she has become one herself. The first red flag was when Paul was convicted of drunk and disorderly conduct back in February 2020, after his behaviour outside Ryan's Bar the previous Christmas. When it had come to court, he had charmed her into adjudicating his case. Stupidly she gave in to his cajoling and she had ensured Paul had gotten off lightly with just a fine of five hundred euro. As if nothing had happened, Paul had returned to work after a short suspension was made even shorter with the onset of the Coronavirus. All serving garda had been called into work to help with the manning of checkpoints and other Covid-related issues.

It was different this time though, just as she thought she could move on, Paul is arrested for breaking and entering an ex-girlfriend's house, whom apparently, he was stalking all along. Ciara is truly horrified by this as Paul seemed to hate this Emma person, whenever he spoke of her. Ciara's horror is intensified by the threats she starts to receive when she refuses to help Paul evade justice this time.

At first she ignored phone calls from his solicitor, Don Long and texts from an unknown number went unanswered. Growing more nervous by the day as his solicitor had heavily hinted in a letter to her that his client cannot guarantee to keep her name out of his past if he ended up with another judge in charge of his case. Having spent her whole life building up her career and believing her marriage had ended because of the long hours and work pressure she was under, she wasn't going to sacrifice all that to see Paul get justice, she relents. Ciara's reputation meant more to her than justice being served.

Things played out fairly well for Paul, given the evidence against him and the number of witnesses to his erratic and unpredictable behaviour. On the final day of the trial, Don Long made a display of handing Judge Ciara Donnelly a letter. As the judge pretended to read from what was a blank page, she raised her head to the courtroom and stated, "I can see from the letter before me that the defendant is suffering from mental health issues, and as stated by his doctor is actively attending counselling to address his condition. Given that I feel the defendant offers no threat to society, I feel a custodial sentence would not be suitable in this case. I therefore, recommend a twelve month suspended sentence and an exclusion order pertaining to Ms Emma O'Brien's workplace and home. Also, I impose a fine of three thousand euro in lieu of thirty days in prison. It must not be underestimated that the loss of the defendant's career is a hefty form of punishment also."

Paul was happy with the outcome. As for the fine, he didn't have to pay—Ciara covered it for the promise of silence about her involvement.

Heading to her ensuite bathroom, Ciara spots the box of black hair dye, sitting on the bathroom shelf. Running out of patience waiting for the hairdressers to reopen, she resigns herself to dying her own hair. For the first time in her life, she won't be getting a professional to do it and she is planning to go dark for a change.

Chapter 2
Love in a Bubble

"Do you think I need to colour my hair; can you see any greys coming through?" Jenny is absentmindedly pulling strands of her long dark hair in front of her face to check for greys.

Even though they've not been together that long, Peter knows better than to fall into the trap of telling her that he can indeed see greys and lots of them. Instead, he goes for the safe option, reassuring her, "Your hair looks great to me."

Jenny knows he's being kind and grateful; for the lie, she gives him a broad smile. Allowing Peter to move in with her, when all the lockdowns started, had been a gamble. Knowing living with someone was very different to dating them. Even though they had a short romance before they got engaged at Christmas, Jenny feels like they've known each a lot longer. With the onset of restrictions and various levels of lockdown, time seemed to stretch in an unnatural way. Jenny feels her perception of time is contorted. Regretting her vanity now, she can feel the hair extensions are getting brittle and they feel like little knots in her hair. When she got them in just before Christmas, she didn't realise the way the world would change and the idea of the hairdressers being closed for months on end wasn't even a consideration. For now, she would just have to make do and tie her hair up when she's out in public, like so many others.

Getting up from the breakfast table, Jenny starts to get ready for their daily walk within their neighbourhood. At least the two-kilometre restriction is lifted and they go further afield if they feel like it. But today the sky is grey and a short walk will have to do them. Not knowing how she would have coped if she didn't have Peter, Jenny is continuously surprised by his kindness and his carpentry skills are much appreciated, as her old house seems to be in constant need of his skills.

Having only worked a few months in her new job at Hawes Department Store, Jenny's job ended abruptly last March, when all the shops that were deemed non-essential had locked their doors. Now at home full time with Peter, they were keeping themselves busy with plenty of DIY projects and Jenny was immersing herself into baking banana bread and other new recipes. They joked about gaining the Covid Stone and having to lose weight before their wedding. Agreeing that it would be impossible to even book a date the way things were, they had plenty of time to worry about that.

Jenny doesn't fully grasp just how kind Peter is. Peter knows that Jenny took his brother-in-law's nasty drunken comments to heart. On what turned out to be their last big night out, Paul had gotten himself highly intoxicated and insulted Jenny's personal appearance as well as some weird comments about Jenny's late mother. For peace sake Jenny didn't bring it up again, as Paul was Peter's brother-in-law but it astounded her that someone could even remember her late mother's name, Penny, when they were so out of it.

Even though Peter had assured Jenny that it was just the drink talking, he knows Jenny was very hurt. Things got so bad that night, Paul ended up shouting abuse at everyone at the Christmas party of the Neighbourhood Watch group in the backroom of Ryan's Bar and getting himself arrested. Peter still can't figure out how he got off so lightly.

As they walk out under the dull sky, Peter tries to forget that his sister, Clara, is married to such a nasty man. Not wanting to interfere, Peter has tried to include her in a lot of stuff himself and Jenny are doing. Now that Paul is working as security in that big abandoned hotel, the pressure is some way lifted from Clara, at least she has the place to herself now most nights. Peter knows from being around there the tension levels between Paul and Clara are palpable, so they keep their visits to when Paul is not home.

Following their usual route, they walk past Clara's house. It's a well-appointed three-storey red brick house in an affluent part of the area, Belleview Park. The hanging baskets that frame the front door are perfectly colour co-ordinated and the front windows are gleaming in the sunshine. Neither of them suggests calling in, they know as it's daytime Paul will be there. They walk on in silence, both having the same thought—a perfect but unhappy house.

Chapter 3
We're in the Middle of a Pandemic, You Know!

"Yes, I know we're in the middle of a pandemic, but I'd just like to know if you've made any progress with regards to filing for my divorce." Clara has to try and keep her voice calm, because she knows if she doesn't play nice her solicitor can drag things out even longer. Beginning to suspect that the current pandemic is being used as an excuse for inefficiency, she sighs as she is put on hold for the third time. The dull morning has given way to a sunny afternoon and Clara is absentmindedly watching the dust motes float in the shafts of sunlight.

The narrow windows that line the upper walls of the basement allow in a generous amount of daylight. They afford a chopped off view of the street. Clara can see the mostly sandaled feet of passers-by and can faintly hear their chatter. The weekday footfall has increased during the lockdowns, with people being forced to stay within very short distance of their homes. Despite this, Clara can pick up the almost jovial hellos that now pass between strangers who formerly wouldn't have offered an acknowledgement to each other in the past. Although she knows it's irrational, she feels envious of the more frequent couples that pass her front door they seem to be enjoying this unexpected time being spent together, she knows this will never be the case for her and Paul.

A chirpy voice pulls her back from her ankle watching when it comes back on the line to tell her "Miss Davin is working from home today and can only be contacted by e-mail." Clara thanks the receptionist politely and with a weariness hangs up. Getting back to work, she sends the once languid dust motes into a flurry as she begins to vigorously sand down her latest project. Knowing she is paranoid and that her husband is asleep two floors above her, Clara can't help glancing towards the basement door every couple of minutes. The refurbished basement has become a Godsend during the lockdown, she never spent this much time down here before, but it's a real bolthole for her, as Paul never bothers coming down here.

When they bought the house, the basement was already freshly painted white and had a flagstone floor—so it was perfect for Clara to use as a workshop. Running a charity shop, 'Second Chances', Clara had plenty of opportunity to pick up bric-a-brac for her restoration projects. Most of her handiwork was dotted around the house. Glad now that she a couple of pieces to work on to keep her mind occupied and her creative streak satisfied. She was currently sanding down an old washstand and was trying to decide whether to varnish it or give it a coat of pale blue gloss.

As she crossed the flagstone floor towards the wall shelves to check how much blue paint she had, she heard movement in the kitchen just above her. Immediately on her guard, all sense of creativity left her. Realising that it was later than she thought she glances at her watch and is happy to see it was almost time for Paul to go to work, just another hour and she would have the house to herself. Over the last few months, the couple had established an unspoken routine of avoiding each other. It wasn't ideal in Clara's mind, but at least it was a big enough house. By the time Paul gets home in the morning, Clara will still be fast asleep in the spare room that has become hers.

Clara feels grateful to the teenagers that kept breaking into the Ardview hotel and vandalising it. It made it necessary for the security company to hire Paul and it made her life a lot easier to be rid of him almost every night. It had surprised her initially that anyone would give Paul a job with his record, until she heard it was all nights and not many people would be interested. Given that the Pandemic Unemployment Payment was available, there probably wasn't a lot of competition for the job.

Going to the mini fridge that is perched on the corner of her workbench, Clara hand lingers over the half-finished bottle of Pinot Grigio that is lying on its side on the bottom shelf before helping herself to a can of coke and settles down on the battered leather sofa. Stretching her legs out she picks out a film on Netflix and plugs in her earphones.

On the floor above her Paul is pacing the floor, he too has his earbuds in and couldn't care less about what his wife is up to below him. It doesn't matter how many times he replays the message he realises that his hearing was right the first time. While he had been sleeping one of his co-workers had left a voicemail on his phone and it had given Paul a cold feeling that began at the back of his neck and had spread quickly over his entire body. Despite the abundance of late afternoon sunshine that filled the large kitchen—Paul was frozen to the core. The message was short, but very meaningful—"Penny rang and said she was sorry to miss you, but that she'll catch up with you another time."

Now the fact that Paul had been due to do a shift last night, but a last-minute switch in the rota meant that he didn't have to go in wasn't unusual. But not a lot of people knew that the old landline in the crumbling hotel was still connected, due to the really weak mobile phone reception up there, the security company thought it was wise to keep the landline connected as a backup. It was still using the same number that hotel had back in the day. Paul found that more than a bit creepy. The only Penny that Paul ever knew, was long dead and he was the only one that knew what really happened to her, and Emma of course had rightly suspected his involvement.

Chapter 4
Frontline Worker

A small A5 padded envelope drops onto the mat to join numerous other ones, just inside the front door of 'Second Chances'.

Paul's little business idea had proved very lucrative and after all everyone deserved a second chance as the name says above the door. His ability to justify even his most dishonest behaviour was immense and he usually managed to square things away with his weak conscience. It had occurred to him one morning when listening to the local radio station. At first he was chuckling to himself as he listened to all the old biddies ringing in and complaining about the youngsters that were still well more or less behaving like youngsters. He was listening to the radio in the car as he was leaving the Ardview carpark, to keep himself alert for the short journey home.

Initially, he thought it was a big overreaction and couldn't really see how these house parties could be stopped—after all the guards were busy enough with all these extra checkpoints on the roads. Feeling fairly sick of being asked the same questions by young guards that looked barely old enough to have made their Confirmation, he did his best to try different routes to avoid them himself. Added to this was the humiliation of being stopped and quizzed by some guards that had worked under him at the station, particularly Brown and Doyle. Those two were well below him in rank when he was a serving garda. But that was before. Before he was caught trespassing in Emma O'Brien's house and being very publicly arrested and had to endure the shame of a court case.

Knowing now that most people either shunned him or enjoyed his fall from grace—he did his best to stay in the shadows. Being labelled as a social pariah and a predator was a far cry from the status he had once enjoyed.

Despite his exhaustion, Paul's attention was peaked when one of the callers to the radio show had suggested that Waterport needed more guards on foot patrol in the city, particularly in the areas that were heavily populated with students. By the time Paul parks outside his own house—he knows how to take full advantage of the pandemic and the opportunity to make money from it.

'Bluebell Wood' housing estate was real student land. Situated on the outskirts of Waterport, but within walking distance of the city centre and all its nightlife. At the moment city centre nightlife is non-existent and the young population need to make their own entertainment. This was ripe hunting ground for disgraced ex-garda Paul Lombard.

Paul's wife Clara didn't care that her husband was out every night of the week, she was glad of it. Something was playing on her mind ever since what turned out to be their last night out together the previous Christmas. Still feeling shamed by Paul's drunken state and how he had made an absolute spectacle of himself and her by association. In front of a crowd on one of the busiest nights of the year, Paul had become really abusive to one of his ex-girlfriends, Emma

O'Brien, who also happened to co-own the pub with her mother, Rosie.

The strength of his emotions that night proved to Clara that Paul still had unresolved feelings for Emma. That night had ended up with Paul being arrested for being drunk and disorderly. The most astonishing thing about it all was that not long afterwards Paul was caught hiding in Emma's attic and the whole thing ended in a very public court case and Paul losing his job. Her brother Peter had pointed out to her that Paul had gotten off lightly and had hinted at some kind of special treatment for Paul because of corruption within the ranks. Clara couldn't help thinking the same thing.

Following the trial, Clara had been too embarrassed to go out and did her best to scurry to and from work without being noticed. Once there, she would hide herself in the back office for most of the day. When the lockdown was announced that March, Clara felt a mixture of relief and panic. Relief at not having to see people and panic at having to see Paul more. As things turned out, Paul seemed to be busier than ever, and that suited Clara fine.

In her solitude, Clara had more time than ever to rethink events of recent times, something Paul had said in his belligerent state that night in Ryan's kept bothering her—she didn't mention it to Jenny for fear of upsetting her. Paul had shouted to Emma that it should have been her that he had thrown into the sea. It wasn't the usual stuff drunks came out with. It was both specific and bizarrely random. The only person that Clara could think of that was lost at sea was Jenny's mother, Penny.

Not wanting to believe her husband was capable of such an act, Clara tried to put it out of her mind. It was bad enough being married to a stalker, never mind a murderer. During lockdown she had watched more television than ever, in particular crime solving programmes and the wife was often the last to know, or worse the victim.

While his wife is living in fear and locking her bedroom door at night, Paul is living his best life. The old garda uniform that he had grown too heavy for, was now a perfect fit. It had lain in the back of his wardrobe for years—a reminder of his fondness for fig rolls and all things sweet. He wasn't sure if it was the stress of the court case or all the exercise he was getting on his new 'beat'. Either way Paul was very pleased with the way he looked in his uniform. Admiring his reflection in the front door glass of one of the noisier houses on the estate, Paul inhales deeply and puffs out his chest, just before it's opened by a girl of nineteen at the most. Blearily she asks him if he's seen the pizza guy's delivery van. Replying with a stern no, the girl is about to shut the door with a roll of her eyes, when Paul puts his foot up against it to stop her.

Paul enjoys the look of panic that is spreading across the girl's face as she only now notices his uniform. Paul hasn't bothered with the garda cap, he likes the element of surprise, and the hat brings too much attention. His plan wouldn't work if a member of the public actually called on him for some kind of assistance. Flashing his identity badge in front of the stunned girl's face for a second, he asks her to step outside, and begins his routine.

"Are you having a house party?" he asks in a disgusted voice, the girl doesn't answer, just nods. Almost disappointed that the girl is such a walkover, Paul goes on to tell her that he wants the names and addresses of everyone in the house and that their parents will be contacted. With a disapproving sigh Paul goes on to tell her there is another way to make good on the situation.

Nodding along to Paul's suggestion, the girl re-enters the house and collects money from each partygoer, repeating Paul's threat that anyone who doesn't pay up will have to supply their names to the very reasonable garda standing in the porch. After a few minutes, the girl returns with a bundle of cash, as Paul reassures her that the money will go to charity, he leaves her after issuing a stern warning.

Getting back into his car, he pulls off his facemask, glad at the extra layer of disguise it affords him. 'Bluebell Wood', is so named after the small woods and the abundance of wild bluebells that used to grow in the area, when it was still the countryside. Now the only bluebells apparent are the two painted ones on the entrance sign to the estate. Given its proximity to the third level college in Waterport it has turned into one of those estates mostly rented by students that are from out of town, so the chances of being recognised are even less. Paul has parked at the far end of the estate. A pleased Paul is counting his takings for the night. He can't help laughing out loud at the stupidity of these youngsters. Didn't their parents teach them anything? Why does nobody really look at his ID badge? If they did they would see it was one from his job as a security man, and that he was not a guard! If the future of the world is in the hands of this lot—we were in trouble!

Putting his car into gear, Paul heads towards 'Second Chances' to collect some more 'donations', these ones were more long-term arrangements than the one-off 'fines' that he issued to clueless students. Since losing his job as detective,

Paul was at his most dangerous because he had nothing left to lose.

Throughout his career and more particularly when he was promoted to detective, Paul had both witnessed and benefited from favours and bribes for himself and a certain cohort of his colleagues. For Paul those bribes now presented themselves as blackmail. One by one Paul had contacted his former peers to let them know how exactly he could damage their reputations and how much each of them needed to deposit through the letterbox of 'Second Chances' on a monthly basis to keep their names out of the news.

Coming in through the back door of his house, Paul silently hangs the keys to 'Second Chances' back on the hook in the utility room. Worried that his wife might notice them missing the next time he takes them, he promises himself to get a set cut for himself. So far Clara hasn't noticed them disappear on the second Sunday of every month. Paul knows that nobody ever visits the shop on Sundays, neither staff nor customers. Since lockdown, the chances of being caught are even less. Clara's trusting nature has served Paul well, she even has the alarm code for the shop written on the cat shaped keyring that she keeps them on. Paul needn't have worried, the only pair of eyes on him that night were Ginger the cat's. From his position on the deep window sill, he could see all, and even envies the catlike stealth of Paul.

Chapter 5
Stay Safe—Keep Your Distance

"For the last time, we've been through these enough times now; if they ask we're from the same household, just tell them we're sisters, or even a couple." With this last suggestion, Maura breaks her pace and gives Betty a raised eyebrow. "They won't notice we're not keeping our distance, they're too busy hassling motorists about going to the beach."

Betty is starting to lose her patience with Maura as they have had this same conversation every time they go for a walk in their neighbourhood, and they are well within their restriction zone. Maura knows she's being silly and agrees with her friend with a quiet nod of her head.

The two have been friends since childhood and in truth were more like sisters. Linking arms, they make their way slowly around the streets of Mapleview Estate and comment on the gardens and how well everybody seems to be keeping them. They both know that it's because of the pandemic and people are so bored they are doing a lot more gardening and DIY than usual. It's a beautiful sunny morning and the ladies are enjoying their stroll. Maura is still on the waiting list to get her cataracts done and with all the cancelled elective surgery she has no idea when the operation will go ahead. If she dwells on it, she gets very frustrated and her mood can get very low, there is nothing she can do about it, Betty has proven to be a good friend and a rock for her.

As Maura's eyesight is growing weaker, she has become more nervous about going out for fear of falling, she has never felt more vulnerable. Without Betty, she doesn't know if she would be brave enough to go past her own front gate. Clutching tightly to Betty's arm, Maura feels like she's part of the world again.

As the pair nears the entrance to the housing estate, which opens up onto the main road, Maura feels Betty tense up and without speaking, she is aware of tension in Betty. Briskly and picking up her pace, Betty mutters, "Quick, cross the road!" Assuming that it's one of the garda checkpoints that Maura is so nervous of, she matches Betty's pace and doesn't speak until she feels Betty's arm relax.

"Is it the guards; are they looking at us?" Maura is turning her head in all directions, wondering if her eyes were so bad that she couldn't even see the blur of the guards' high visibility jackets or their squad car. All she can see is a figure in dark clothing, a blur really that is moving away from them in the distance.

"It's your man, that dodgy ex-garda, you know the one that was stalking Emma O'Brien from the pub, remember they found him hiding in her attic," Betty explains in an unnecessary whisper. He was so far away from them now he couldn't possibly overhear them. Paul creeped Betty out so much even talking about him made her nervous, she had to stop herself from making the sign of the cross. Almost immediately she regrets sharing this information with Maura, she should have just lied and told her there was a garda checkpoint and they were staring at them for being too close to each other.

Betty knows the mention of Emma will start another long account of the murder of that old priest in St Patrick's church a while back. Maura seemed to irrationally blame herself for the whole thing—just because she had cleaned the confession box that morning, but couldn't one hundred per cent say if she would have noticed the suspect's supermarket loyalty card there before the murder had taken place. Even though Maura claimed her eyesight wasn't that bad at the time, she had to admit to the guards that it was possible in the gloom of the confessional she may have missed it. This Maura believed is what got Emma O'Brien off with murder.

Maura didn't know that after being blackmailed by Emma, Paul Lombard has actually 'lost' the only piece of evidence—the supermarket loyalty card with Emma's name on it—in a bid to cover up his own part in a local woman, Penny Power's disappearance (assumed drowning) back in 1990.

Betty has to stop herself from sighing with exasperation when Maura right on que, begins her usual account of what she thinks of that 'Emma one'. Not for the first time Betty has to remind her of being innocent until proven guilty and tries to change the subject. But Maura isn't finished yet and asks Betty if she thinks the two of them were in it together—some kind of cover up. Not really sure what to make of this, Betty thinks back to what turned out to be their last night out in Ryan's Bar and the awful abuse Paul Lombard was shouting at Emma, before he got himself arrested for being drunk and disorderly. He had really made a show of himself. Whatever had gone on between the two of them, there was definitely unfinished business.

As they turn the bend that will bring them the full circle and back to where they started, the two ladies agree that it's Paul's wife Clara that they feel sorry for. Remembering that night in the pub, the poor woman was mortified. Betty and Maura both liked Clara, whenever they had met in the charity shop, she was always so friendly. "I don't know what she sees in that fella, he was always full of himself," Maura comments, just as she and Betty reach her front door.

Agreeing, Betty nods adding, "They live in one of the most beautiful houses in town—you never know what goes on behind closed doors, do you?"

The subject of ladies' conversation hadn't even noticed them, he is hurrying head bent along the road, distracted by a picture that has appeared on his mobile phone. It's in his text messages and is from an unknown number. The picture is a beautiful scenery shot take on a glorious day. Its location is Gull Cove. Paul's mind is racing now as he does a mental list of any possible people that may have witnessed him throwing Penny Power's body into the sea there decades earlier and why now they would choose to reveal it. It was the kind of picture that a good photographer or an artist would take to work on sketches of. After walking in circles for almost an hour, when he arrives back at his own front door, there is only one name that keeps popping into his head—Emma.

Chapter 6
Working from Home

Emma has done everything, but nothing is coming to her today. The most annoying thing about this is ideas pop into her head when she is too busy to sit down and write. Sometimes when she is just about to drop off to sleep, she will think of something. If she doesn't sit up and write them down in one of her many notebooks that are scattered here and there around the house, she will forget it by the next morning. Today though she is determined to finish chapter six, despite going for her usual walk and drinking three cups of coffee, her mind is too fuzzy to get into the writing zone. Last night's disagreement with her mother Rosie had annoyed her and she hadn't slept properly.

The previous evening, she had handed her mother the first five finished chapters to read in the upstairs apartment of Ryan's, the pub they co-owned and had sat back waiting for her mother's reaction. While her mother was reading, Emma flicked through the television channels with the sound muted. Emma wasn't watching her mother's face as she got deeper into the chapters. If she had been, she might have noticed her mother's look of horror and Emma would have been forewarned of her mother's reaction.

"You can't write THAT!" Rosie's voice was raised, which in itself was unusual. Rosie was a quiet ladylike woman—quite different to her daughter. Rosie had just finished reading and has thrown the short manuscript down onto the coffee table with obvious revulsion.

Emma is shocked, she had expected praise, and immediately goes on the defensive—she was very sensitive about her writing, and this was something that she had wanted to do for a long time; she retorts—"I can write what I like—what's wrong with it?" The question was genuine, Emma was really so self-unaware she couldn't see anything but good and sharp writing with a smattering of her wit thrown in. Emma was very proud of her work so far and she would defend it ferociously.

Rosie realises quickly that Emma really doesn't see a problem in writing about the disappearance of a local woman in a thinly veiled setting that resembles Waterport. Even in this if you looked quickly at the fictional town name—Waterpoint, you would think it was Waterport. In all, Emma has only completed five chapters fully at this point and has managed to implicate herself. There is a strong male character that Emma has named Paud, which is so obviously Paul Lombard, Emma's ex-boyfriend from years back, who currently has a restraining order served on him by the court. The physical description for 'Paud' is a double for Paul.

Emma has even given 'Paud' a wife that fits Paul Lombard's wife Clara's description perfectly. Claudia is the name chosen by Emma for this 'fictional' character. Rosie also notes that poor 'Claudia' has been painted in an unflattering light and Emma has done nothing to highlight the woman's good looks. The main character however, 'Ella', is generously described as the local beauty and quite the head-turner.

Rosie is bewildered by her daughter's capability for stirring up trouble and yet playing the innocent at all times. Fearful now that Emma is actually serious about going ahead with this book, Rosie has to admit it does make good reading and if it wasn't so close to home, it's a book that she herself might enjoy. Rosie tries to play on Emma's vanity and tells her that the writing is just too good. Some people around here just won't get that it's a product of her imagination and not some sort of admission of guilt. Feeling bad about her negativity, Rosie tries to lighten things by saying, "If Agatha Christie lived around here, some of our customers would think she was a serial killer, just because she wrote about murder." But this doesn't raise a smile from Emma and Rosie knows Emma won't give up so easily.

Arguing that the description of the beach and its surrounding area are too similar to Gull Cove, the last known whereabouts of Penny Power, the real missing woman from Waterport is too much of a coincidence. Reassuring Emma that even though she knows Emma wouldn't be involved in such a thing—others might believe she is writing from first-hand experience; Rosie tries to explain calmly to Emma. At first Rosie thinks she is winning Emma around, because a big smile is spreading across Emma's face, and she is nodding along to this. Believing that she can has gotten through to Emma, Rosie goes on to tell her, "This writing thing is too much like hard work anyway, why don't you go back to your painting if you're bored. This pandemic has us all driven up the wall—you just need another outlet."

Ignoring her mother's patronising tone, Emma replies smugly, "You're right of course, my descriptive skills are very good, and I'll take that as a compliment. They say good writing should make the reader a little uncomfortable and going on your reaction, I think I'll have a success on my hands with this little book of mine."

Emma's reply has left Rosie stunned and before Rosie can stop herself, she looks Emma in the eye and exclaims, "People will think Paul is a murderer and you were in on it."

Expecting a backlash from Emma, Rosie holds her breath and braces herself. Emma merely replies in a chillingly cold way to her mother, "Don't be silly, it's only fiction after all." Before she flounces out of the room, clasping her chapters tightly to her chest.

Glancing at her watch, Emma decides to shake off last night's negativity, and helps herself to another coffee. Treating herself to a proper Americano from her new coffee machine—she trots back to her desk with renewed vigour. After a quick read through of her handwritten notes, Emma settles herself in front of her laptop and begins to type. Having mulled over her mother's comments, she has settled into her next chapter—they say you should write about what you know. Chapter six goes into the effects of being adopted as a baby has had on Ella and being raised by an alcoholic while your birth mother hides away and watches from a distance. A few hours have passed by the time Emma realises that she's hungry and decides to look at her muted phone. There are three missed calls from Rosie, before Emma rings her back she has lunch. Finally, she calls her mother's number. The conversation is short, barely two minutes long. It finishes by

Emma tersely telling Rosie, "No, I won't be over today, I'm working from home."

Rosie knows better than to contact Emma for a couple of days and has resigned herself to spending the time Emma needs to calm down alone. So, it was almost a relief, later in the week when she heard the front door of the pub downstairs being unlocked. Rosie was still in the process of dressing herself and she could hear Emma's voice as she was climbing the stairs to Rosie's apartment.

"Where are you going?"

"Where are you coming from?"

"What is the purpose of your journey? For God's sake, if those two eejits ask me the same three questions again, I'm going to scream!"

Rosie knows exactly who Emma is shouting about and doesn't need to ask if it's the two newly recruited guards that are stationed at the end of the road asking everybody the same questions. Feeling sorry for the two youngsters, Rosie attempts to reason with Emma that the poor lads are only doing their jobs and are probably getting abused by people on a daily basis. Emma has flung three bags of groceries onto the countertop and has flicked the kettle on, quickly changing the subject Rosie tells her not to bother putting the groceries away, as she wants to clean them first.

"What do you mean, clean them first?" Emma genuinely thought she has misheard her mother, not an unusual thing as she was hard of hearing.

"I was just listening to Adrian Geary on the local radio show, and he said it's now recommended to wipe down all your shopping with antibacterial wipes before putting them away," Rosie responds sheepishly; she knows Emma thinks a lot of these Covid rules and regulations are nonsense, and immediately regrets sharing this bit of new advice with her daughter.

Emma slams the fridge door with unnecessary force and fires back, "What next, I've heard it all now, you should know better, Mother. Adrian Geary should be called Aimless and Dreary, I don't know why you still listen to that doomsayer, you be better off turning off the radio and listening to a good podcast."

Rosie knows that Emma only calls her 'Mother' when she is getting wound up and tries to change the subject again from all Covid talk.

"What have you been up to for the last couple of days?" Rosie asks gently.

Emma is taken aback by this question and had assumed her mother would realise that she was busy writing her book.

"I've been working from home as they call it these days and I'm exhausted," comes the mysterious reply from Emma.

"Ah that's good, I'm glad you've dropped the book thing and got on with some real work. You were always handy with a paintbrush. What room are you working on? When you're finished, you could paint my bedroom if you're feeling energetic."

Rosie tries to hide the relief in her voice, and is shocked when Emma barks back, "Firstly, I am a landscape and portrait artist, not a housepainter, and WRITING IS REAL WORK!"

Chapter 7
M (Asking for a Friend)

In the beginning of the pandemic, Margo was loving this new sense of purpose it had given her and the bright pink high visibility vest that she got to wear. Being head of the Neighbourhood Watch group was as empowering as this is. Even though she is part of a team of volunteers in the locality, checking up on the elderly people that were 'cocooning', Margo felt like she was in charge and automatically assumed the role of boss. Already irritating the other volunteers, some of whom were already familiar with her domineering ways from being in the Neighbourhood Watch group with her, Margo proved to be equally forceful with the people they were supposed to be helping.

Fr Darragh dreads his meet ups with Margo, since the churches have reopened on a scaled back version, she has been tormenting him with phone calls and 'rules', she seems to be making up herself. First it was the ridiculous signs everywhere, even in the most unnecessary places and who was going to get all the sticky glue residue off the seats and the flooring when all this was over, if it ever was. Margo insisted on ushering the few church goers to their seats in a most authoritarian manner, the priest was afraid she would frighten off people.

On top of that, church collections were almost non-existent, except for online donations, Fr. Darragh doesn't know how he could keep the heating on in the church. Somehow, he has gotten himself into a regular outdoor meeting, with at least a six foot gap between them, in the church grounds with Margo every Friday morning to 'discuss', how to manage all the new protocol that was necessary to hold Mass at the weekend. Knowing this will end up with Margo simply bossing him around and lecturing him on the importance of using hand gel at Communion time and leaving his mask on at all times, all of which he has heard before. Fr. Darragh wishes the Neighbourhood Watch group could start meeting up again soon, as he knows he's just a poor substitute for Margo's power trip, and then he might get some peace.

"I'll be back in about an hour, Fr Darragh needs me," Margo shouts over her shoulder in the direction of the sitting room as she puts on her mask and pink high visibility jacket.

Jack her husband gives a contented sigh and flicks on the television remote as he mutters, "Thank God for that." Throwing his feet up on the sofa.

Margo doesn't really need the high visibility jacket that she's put on, but she feels it gives her an air of authority and for now that seems to be all she has. Since the lockdowns and limited levels of freedom that the world has experienced Margo feels a gaping hole in her life. Up to now she was a very active member of the community and was always very generous with her time by way of volunteering and organising local fund raisers and different events.

On a deeper level, Margo knows that the community work was really filling a void in her life, since she retired as a primary school teacher. She hadn't realised how much she would miss the routine of her working life and has striven to fill most evenings with activities that got her out of the house. Margo doesn't know that her enthusiasm and organisational skills were often viewed by others as being bossy and a bit controlling. It's only beginning to occur to her now, that without the organised routine of such things as the Neighbourhood Watch meetings and her parish council work, she didn't really have much contact with people, and is feeling the sharp knife of loneliness deeper by the day.

Much fuss had been made in the early days of the pandemic of keeping your distance from each other and Margo noticed on her walk to the church, more and more people that she knew weren't from the same household were gathering for outdoor cups of coffee and walks. As she was leaving her own house, she had seen Betty and Martha linking each other and having a good old natter. If she was paranoid she may have been offended when they crossed the street as she was heading in their direction, but Margo put it down to nervousness about catching Covid. Only for they had returned her wave, she would have thought they hadn't seen her.

As she passed through the public park, she felt briefly heartened by the sunshine that was starting to get stronger as the day progressed. As she took in her surroundings, she could see at least four of her fellow parish council members sitting around one of the picnic tables and drinking what she assumed to be coffee from those paper cups, even from her vantage point at the opposite side of the pond she could hear the cheerful chatter and hearty laughter from their table. In the hope she might be invited to join them, she gave them an exaggerated wave, and headed in their direction. As she neared the table, and they became aware of her, the laughter and chatter died down to an awkward silence.

Eventually, one of the more outspoken of the group, Liz, bid Margo a good morning, it was more of a dismissal than a friendly greeting or invitation and turned back to the group to continue their conversation. Liz was a sharp-featured woman in her sixties, with greying mousy hair, and was definitely the ringleader, the others almost feared her as much as they liked her. Briefly, Margo just stood there, and before she could stop herself announced, "I can't stop, I have a very important meeting with the parish priest."

At least the assembled group had the decency to wait until Margo was out of earshot before they descended into laughter. They had found it funny that Margo was wearing a mask outdoors. As the park gate squeakily swung out behind her, the starkness of being friendless hit Margo as she wearily climbed the hill towards the church.

As Fr Darragh was leaving the sanctuary of the Sacristy, and silently praying for rain to end his 'outdoor meeting' with Margo early, he could hear someone shuffling around near the noticeboard that was in the small hallway between the main church and the Sacristy door. It was Margo, of course, she was taking a photograph of the poster for the 'Together', voluntary group, that offered counselling to people suffering from depression or loneliness and needing someone to talk to.

Margo seemed startled to see the priest standing next to her and mumbled in a low voice, she might offer her services and she knew a couple of people that might need their help, the priest didn't really think much of it, and they continued to the bench that was sitting just outside the church door. Sitting at opposite ends, of course, Margo was strangely quiet. Instead of her usual bluster, the priest found her to be preoccupied and almost downhearted. Bracing himself, Fr Darragh, asked Margo if everything was alright, and if there was anything he could help her with. Being such a strong and formidable woman, the priest was half expecting a retort or some kind rebuff for his offer of help. Instead, Margo just stood up slowly and bade the priest a subdued goodbye.

Taking the long way home and avoiding the park, Margo stole another glance at her phone. Hoping that it was simply a mistake that she wasn't included in any of the outdoor social arrangements that appeared to be going on without her, her heart fell when again there were no text messages inviting her along to the next meet up. Feeling bitterness creep into her heart, she sat down heavily on one of the stone benches that lined the quayside of Waterport.

A good hour had passed when Margo finally lifted her eyes from hypnotic ebb and flow of the river Óir flying past her and the gloaming had settled in around her. The evening air had brought a dampness and slight mist to the quayside. The pleasure crafts, that bobbed on the far side of the river were now thrown into silhouette, the normally pristine and well cared for seacrafts of varying sizes and values were now looking neglected and had started to take on the greenish hue of algae. Their owners now forbidden to make unnecessary journeys were unable to attend to and use their boats. Margo didn't notice this or the dark masked figure that scurried past her on his way to 'Second Chances'. Finally roused by the encroaching darkness Margo reluctantly pulled out her mobile phone from her pocket and dialled the number of the

'Together' support group, not offering her help as a volunteer when she got through but seeking their help as a client.

Chapter 8
"A Meaningful Christmas"
December 2020

"It's a sign, I'm telling you." Jenny is looking out her kitchen window at the robust, red-breasted robin hungrily pecking away at the fat ball that Jenny has left on the bird table.

"No, it's a sign that you left out some bird food," comes the sarcastic reply from the kitchen table, Peter is trying to listen to the news headlines on the radio. He starts sighing to himself at the nonsense talk of the politician being interviewed about how restrictions were going to be eased for the Christmas period and that everyone should be looking forward to a meaningful Christmas.

Jenny goes on to explain the old legend of the robin being a deceased loved one coming back with a message.

"How can you even tell if it's the same bird?" replies Peter with a barely concealed grin.

"Well, I can't, I just feel it," Jenny replies defensively.

Jenny's instincts usually served her well, except when it came to Peter's brother-in-law, Paul Lombard, she knows now that she had gotten that one spectacularly wrong. Initially she had confided in Paul and had even trusted him with her late mother Penny's private journal, hoping that he may be help her find out what really happened to her. Penny had been missing for decades and it was genuinely believed locally that she had simply drowned while swimming alone at Gull Cove. Jenny however believed foul play was involved and in recent years had felt strongly enough to ask Paul for help in reopening the case.

At the time Paul was a serving detective and was highly thought of. Now, though Paul is a disgraced ex-garda, having been convicted of drunk and disorderly conduct just last Christmas at Ryan's Bar. This was to be hotly followed on St Patrick's Day by breaking and entering as well as stalking his ex-girlfriend, Emma O'Brien.

Jenny had even gone so far as suggest Paul may have played a part in her mother's disappearance to Peter recently, as Paul had been shouting about Penny when he was drunk. Peter had told her to reign in her imagination, he couldn't entertain the idea that his sister might be married to a murderer, as well as a stalker and all-round creep. These suspicions had crossed Peter's mind also, but he couldn't admit it to Jenny, as he knew there was nothing they could do to prove it, not legally anyway. Paul had even managed to 'misplace' Penny's old journal that could have held some clues to any possible suspects.

Jenny is staring out the window all the while her mind is mulling over the rapid fall from grace Paul Lombard has taken and her thoughts turn to Christmas Day, as it suddenly occurs to her that she might end up spending it with Clara and Paul. Turning to Peter quickly she asks if Paul is working over Christmas Day, and a reassuring Peter tells her he is and that it'll just be Clara sharing the day with them, and Clara is happy to do the cooking. Without any pretence, Jenny gives a relieved sigh and visibly relaxes.

Peter sees this and makes her laugh when he jokes, "It can't be any worse than last Christmas, after the show Paul made of us in Ryan's."

They both agree that Christmas will be much better without Paul around.

Christmas is the last thing on Paul's mind as he lets himself into 'Second Chances' and efficiently makes his way to the alarm box in the back office. Experience has taught him not to put the overhead lights on and to manage with the light from his mobile phone. With catlike movements he makes his way back to entrance and retrieves his usual stash of envelopes, each with a number written on the outside. Paul is quite proud of his accounting skills, he has devised a system that should anyone come across the envelopes, they would just see his name on them and a meaningless number that wouldn't incriminate his 'clients'.

For each person he is blackmailing, he has a corresponding number in his little black notebook that he keeps on him at all times, he doesn't want that book falling into the wrong hands. He even sleeps with it under his pillow for fear of his wife, Clara finding it. There was no chance of that though, Clara never went into the bedroom he slept in. The most intriguing envelope almost goes unnoticed, it had fallen at an angle and had caught on the draught excluder that ran along the bottom of the old shop door. It was different from the other brown or buff envelopes, this one was pink and had his name in handwritten thatched writing that was in itself a work of art. Paul knew this one was written with a light feminine hand and when he lifted it from the floor, it had a faint floral scent that was somehow familiar to him.

For reasons unknown even to himself, Paul handled this envelope with reverence, it seemed wrong to tear it open greedily like he had with the other ones. Instead, he hesitated briefly and held it to his nose and slowly inhaled the scent again, breathing deeply he felt a mixture of familiarity that soon gave way to a deep dread that was churning in the pit of his stomach.

Paul gave a shiver when he finally read the contents of the pretty pink envelope. It simply stated, "We'll be together soon, Penny." The handwriting was the same beautiful script that matched the writing on the exterior of the envelope. This message disturbed him more than the last one that was delivered by post. It seemed more personal as it was handwritten, and it also meant whoever was behind it knew he visited the shop regularly and that meant they knew about his little blackmailing business too.

By the time Paul makes it back to his own house, he is shaking and heads straight up to his bedroom; like a sulky teenager, he slams the door and throws himself onto the bed. In a bid to calm himself, he turns on the television that is sitting on the chest of drawers opposite his bed. It was impossible to concentrate on the current affairs programme that is running, and the politician suggesting to put Granny near an open window to eat her Christmas dinner and not share the gravy boat, just washes over him as he flops onto his back and gazes at the ceiling with a panicked look in his eyes.

Chapter 9
Virtual Learning?
Early 2021

"She wants to be called 'Pol' now, if you don't mind; she should have kept her grandmother's name Penelope or even Polly was better than this! Pol sounds like a streetwalker's name."

Peter looks up at Jenny in puzzlement and surprise, it's not like her to have a bad word to say about her favourite niece and goddaughter. Sensing it's more to do with a feeling of disrespect towards Jenny's late mother, Penny, he decides to stay silent. Jenny has just hung up from talking to her sister-in-law Tess and after a lengthy conversation feels both pity and irritation for her niece. In truth, Polly looked more like her daughter than her niece, sharing the same dark colouring, but as Polly had gotten older her build was more petite and slender than Jenny's, sometimes it shocked Jenny at how alike Polly and Penny were.

Defiantly announcing to Peter that she was still going to call her Polly and she could get over it. At least she could understand how the pet name had come about, when her niece was small her brother Seán couldn't pronounce Penelope and her name had morphed into Polly, in favour of the nursery rhyme that played constantly on the baby mobile that had hung over her crib. As she got older Polly was playfully teased by her family to 'put the kettle on', whenever they wanted a cup of tea.

Over the phone, Tess had unintentionally offloaded onto Jenny all the woes of having teenagers at home all day from school and the trouble with having a poor Wi-Fi signal. "It was alright for the bigwig politicians up in Dublin, insisting that 'life is online now'. They should come down to Ferrybranch when they are all online at once for classes—it would drive you mad."

Ferrybranch was across the bridge from the main shopping area of Waterport and Jenny could see how its infrastructure could be a bit left behind. Although it was named after both the ferries that used to bring people to England directly from the quayside and the train line that used to branch Eastward from Waterport, both are now part of local history, and in some ways Ferrybranch had been much forgotten in terms of local investment. It didn't help that the once thriving Ardview Hotel, was laying in tatters up in the cliffside that forms the main entrance to the locality, as you cross the bridge.

"That crowd up in the Dáil haven't a clue what it's like outside The Pale." Despite the bitterness of Tess's tone, Jenny gave a giggle at the old-fashioned term used to refer to anywhere in The Republic outside of Dublin. Tess was on a roll now and didn't even notice Jenny's soft laugh. Barely stopping for breath, Tess had gone on to say how worried she was about Polly and where she was going with her friends in the evenings. As all the usual activities for the teenagers are closed because of Covid for the foreseeable future, Tess can't stop her daughter from meeting her friends for walks.

With Covid figures gone through the roof after our 'meaningful Christmas', there's not much chance of them going back to school soon. It's the only contact that she gets with her friends, what worries Tess is state of Polly's clothes when she sees them as she loads the washing machine. They are caked in mud and there are even a few tears in the new pair of jeans that she only got delivered last week. What's worrying Tess more though is the faint smell of smoke, a smell that reminds Tess of bonfire nights years ago, when it wasn't illegal in Ireland to have one. When Tess declares, that Green crowd have a lot to answer for, at least if it was an organised one it might be safer, Jenny thinks she has finished and wants to say her goodbyes, but she allows Tess to continue as she knows it's doing her good to get it off her chest.

Not wanting to end their conversation on a negative tone, Tess goes on to tell Jenny, "I suppose it could be worse, there could be a smell of pot from her clothes and gives a nervous, high-pitched laugh. At least I don't have to worry about Seán, he has his music to keep him busy, thank God one of them is no bother."

Normally, these conversations between Jenny and Tess would be held in one of the local cafes when the teenagers in questions were at school and well out of earshot. What Tess doesn't realise is that Polly is standing at the top of the stairs and has been listening to the whole of Tess's side of the phone call. Tess had been in the hall keeping an eye out for the delivery man from the supermarket when she had answered the call from Jenny. Absentmindedly, she had plonked herself onto the second last step of the stairs, it was a good vantage point to see anyone coming up the driveway, and she was oblivious to the listener on the landing above her.

The delivery man arrives just as Tess has ended her phone call and leaves the groceries in the front porch. Putting on latex gloves, that Tess has in her back pocket, at the ready, she goes out to retrieve them, so she doesn't even hear the angry slam of Polly's bedroom door.

Tutting to herself as she hauls the groceries in and lifts them up onto the kitchen counter, she has called up the stairs a couple of times to Polly for help with putting away the shopping and has been ignored. "Why does nobody ever listen to me?" she asks herself and begins the task of fastidiously checking the condition of her fruit and vegetables before putting them away.

Polly allows herself another eyeroll as she can hear her mother's voice bellowing the wrong lyrics of one of her favourites songs from the kitchen. "Save your beers for another day." Tess cheerfully repeats at full blast as she busies herself with sanitising the rest of the groceries.

One thing Tess is right about is the pathetic wi-fi in the whole of the Ferrybranch area. Paul pulling out his earphones has abandoned his laptop and the docuseries he's been following online. He now decides to do the word puzzle on his phone that has become so popular since people are living such limited lives. Paul usually completes it in three attempts and tonight is no different. Leaning back in the old leather swivel chair that's behind the now redundant reception desk, he stretches and wonders how he's going to fill the next eight hours of his shift in Ardview Hotel.

With his thoughts now turning to Emma as they inevitably always do, he goes momentarily cold when he thinks of the note he found in 'Second Chances'. It's now in his jacket pocket and he takes it out again to inhale the scent. The familiarity of it has been bothering him and he can't quite place it. Not being an expert on perfume, he decides the significance of it is lost on him and can only assume the sender overestimates his sense of smell.

By the time Tommy, Paul's co-worker emerges from his snooze in the back office, it's well past midnight and he's wondering why Paul is laughing to himself. The office is behind the reception desk, so Tommy can only see Paul from behind but he sees his shoulders shaking with laughter as he approaches. It's only when Tommy goes around to the front of the desk, does Paul notice him and with a start he pulls out his earphones that are now attached to his phone. Asking Paul what it is that's so funny Paul explains about the playback radio programme he's listening too. Apparently, some politicians up in the midlands were caught having a leaving party for one of their colleagues. "The cheek of those hypocrites," Paul almost shouts at Tommy.

Paul decides to go for a smoke outside before he goes for his nap, and is glad he had brought his earphones to work that night, otherwise the boredom would have been unbearable. If Paul hadn't brought them though he might have heard the footsteps that were moving above him on the first floor while he was engrossed in the radio programme. The dislodged sheet of plywood that had been covering where a large pane of glass was missing from the old bar area of the hotel might have been noticed too, if Paul and Tommy had bothered to do their jobs properly. But each wrongly assumed the other was at least doing one patrol a night.

Paul settles himself on one of the round outdoor picnic tables with attached seats outside the hotel just under what was left of the awning and reaches into his pocket for his lighter. The remaining fabric panels of the umbrella over Paul's table promoting a well-known cider is in rags and the only remaining letters spell out BUMER. Instead of feeling the hard plastic of his lighter, Paul is repulsed when he feels something soft and snakelike in shape. With a sharp intake of breath Paul pinches the organic like material between his index finger and thumb and quickly throws it onto the ground, almost expecting it to slither away.

Paul has a paralysing fear of creepy crawlies and rodents. At first it looks like a long black worm of some type, and only after kicking it a few times does Paul realise it's not alive. What Paul finds himself staring at is a clump of long thick black hair, that confuses and disgusts him simultaneously.

Paul had in a way reconciled himself to believing Emma was the source of his torment, he had made peace with it. Emma had proved to be similar to himself, and he knew she would have too much to lose if she exposed Paul for his part in Penny Power's disappearance. In a way he was flattered when he thought Emma was thinking about him, she was after all living rent free in his head.

But there is only one person in Paul's romantic past with long black hair, and it's not Emma—it was Penny Power.

Chapter 10
Look Out for Each Other

The sky above Gull Cove was a beautiful mixture of pinks, blues and yellows. Above Emma's head, the seagulls were swopping and diving in a hypnotic and rhythmic flow that was distracting and graceful to watch. Emma is perched up on the marram covered sand dunes that look directly down at the Cove. The beach is empty except for a blurry bundle of bright coloured clothes and a pink beach towel strewn among the other belongings of a swimmer that had disappeared into the wide blue ocean.

Feeling around in her bag, Emma's fingers brush against the hard plastic of her ruler and her fingernails catches the remaining crumbs of the blaas (a local type of soft and floury bap) from her previous trips out to sketch on these same hills. Just as her fingers grip her pencils, she sees a figure in the distance. At first, it's a blur of black moving in and out of sight as it negotiates the rolling hills of the sand dunes, but as Emma's eyes stay locked in that direction, the figure becomes clearer and eventually recognisable. Emma tries to call out but finds herself voice taken by a sudden gust of wind and as the figure looms up on top of her, she doesn't even manage a scream as his fingers close tightly around her neck.

Emma bolts upright in bed, and frantically looks around her. Nightmares are not a thing that Emma is usually troubled by. Usually, her nights are undisturbed by conscience or worry and she sleeps like a baby. Rubbing her face, she tries to make sense of it—she recognises the similarity of the location and the significance of it. It was from an almost identical day back in May 1990, when she inadvertently witnessed Paul Lombard running away from the beach—the same day that Penny Power went missing, while swimming there. It had been assumed that she had simply drowned, and her body had been washed out to sea—not the first time this would have happened to swimmers in the area.

A couple of years later, while Emma was in a relationship with Paul, she had figured out he was responsible for Penny's death and had used this to blackmail him when she was a suspect in the stabbing of a local priest. Paul had 'lost' vital evidence that had placed her at the scene. As a result, the case against Emma had been dropped—but there would always be a connection between the two of them.

It made sense to Emma then that the face of her would be strangler was that of Paul's. Despite herself, she had to admit that he still occupied her thoughts a bit too much. If Emma had believed in such things, she might have seen the dream as a premonition, but she didn't believe in all that stuff and put it down to being stuck in the house too much and being overly absorbed in the book she was writing. Instead, it gave her food for thought and jumping out of bed, she headed straight for the bathroom and a hot shower.

Treating herself to a fry up as she had a long day ahead, Emma started gathering up her art materials. Instead of making her nervous that dream had inspired Emma to get back into her sketching, she had neglected her gift for too long. Maybe the dream might be an idea for her next chapter. The book was coming along to her satisfaction, but she seemed to be experiencing what the experts called 'writer's block', at the moment. Some fresh air might do the trick of getting her brain back in gear. As well as packing the usual snacks and art supplies, Emma also loaded her car boot with two bags of dry groceries. It was just as well, as the two young garda that stopped her on the way to Gull Cove asked if her journey was essential, to which she answered sharply, "Of course it is! I have groceries for my elderly mother in the boot!"

Emma and Paul were really more alike than either of them wanted to admit. Emma's dream was not too far off one of the options Paul had been considering for her. The trouble was getting near her to carry it out. Lockdown had made it more difficult to 'bump' into her or get her alone. Not only was Paul subject to a restraining order that banned him from being anywhere near her, but he also knew he would be a suspect if anything happened to her. Now more than ever, he needed to respect the rules of the order. The last thing he wanted was to be seen with someone that will soon be gone missing.

The long black strands of hair that he had found in his pocket had thrown Paul at first, besides it obviously not being the same colour as Emma's, he couldn't think of anyone else that would understand it's meaning. Even though he wished he could hate her, it would make things easier—he knew deep down that he was in love with her. After racking his brains as to who else would be devious and clever enough to know how to rattle him—he could only keep coming to the same answer—Emma.

Somehow she had managed to plant the hair in his pocket, she would be responsible for the letter in Second Chances—he begrudgingly admits that she was capable of anything. To underestimate Emma would be a mistake, on his drive up the long and snaking hillside that leads to Ardview Hotel that evening Paul decides whatever way he ends her, it will be up close and personal—he'd like to look into those wide violet blue eyes one more time before they are closed forever. Emma needs to know who her killer is, before he kisses her goodbye.

On a more practical level, Paul has decided, if he times the tides right, Emma can join Penny in a watery grave. Another thing the two women would have in common, as well as being his victims they were both ex-girlfriends of his. The only difference is that Paul loved Emma. Lost in his thoughts Paul doesn't even notice the song playing on the radio—it's an old Scottish folk song dating back hundreds of years—'My Bonnies Lies over the Ocean'. Paul usually likes the selection of music that the classical station plays, but when his ears finally register the lyrics, he stabs at the off button with more force than is necessary.

Even though Paul knows better than to underestimate Emma, she herself underestimates her physic abilities and is oblivious to the danger she may be in. Instinct had served her well in the past, her late half-sister Essie had found some of Emma's predictions chilling. More than once, Essie had wondered if Emma was some kind of witch and had even called her one to her face a couple of times if they were having a row. Essie had never gotten the upper hand with her younger half-sister. Emma had been adopted by their parents when she was a toddler.

In later years, it had been discovered that Essie's father was Emma's father too—through an affair with Rosie. This had shocked everybody the only one that seemed unphased was Emma, in fact on the last night of Essie's life they had argued viciously about it. The argument ended in Emma screeching at Essie, "The good news is at least my mother isn't an alcoholic and is still alive!" before maniacally laughing at a stunned Essie. These were the last words Essie heard, the last thing she heard was Emma's laughter descending into a cackle as she abruptly turned and slammed the door as she left the room.

Essie hardly ever crosses Emma's mind these days, but she is looking for someone to base one of her characters on. The character is question is a meek and somewhat downtrodden woman with mousy hair and of equally mousey weak character. Not a bit like Emma then.

When Emma finally sits down at her laptop that evening, she is feeling refreshed and inspired. The break from being indoors had really helped her creative juices to flow. It's one o'clock in the morning by the time she finishes the epilogue and with a satisfied grin presses the save button. Tomorrow, she would submit it to the few publishers that are accepting submissions and keep her fingers crossed. Even though she should be exhausted and relaxed now that the book is finally finished, she feels restless and can't sleep—this is unusual for her.

It doesn't take her long to realise why she feels so unsettled, the previous night's dream is coming back into focus for her. Although she doesn't fear that Paul will kill her—he is erratic and unpredictable when he has drink taken, he is a loose cannon. The information he has on her would not just take him down for destroying evidence it would bring her down too. Finally recognising the dream as a warning and registering her gut feeling, she realises she will have to do more about Paul to ensure his silence.

Chapter 11
Unprecedented Times
Summer 2021

The grease is starting to congeal into a slimy puddle under the barbeque leg and is threatening to start sliding towards the wicker chairs that are now occupied by tipsy diners. Of course, it shouldn't have been like this. A couple of years back when Tess had thought about celebrating her and Tim's silver wedding, she had planned a big bash in the Tower Bridge Hotel, just as the name suggested, across the bridge.

The Ardview would have been much nearer, but that was closed for years now with no sign of it opening, she knew they would have to pick somewhere across the bridge on the town side. Tess had even considered renewing their vows, she would have loved the whole thing, but Tim was having none of it. There was no way, as he put it, "that he was putting himself through making a speech again!"

When Tess thought about it, she remembered how nervous and pale he was about the speech on their wedding day and agreed it might a bit much. A big party though that would have been great craic.

The hotel was booked for late April 2020 and the deposit was paid. Once it was booked, Tess relaxed and didn't think she would have anything to worry about, except what to wear, of course. In a way she was right—there was nothing to worry about—because there was nothing, no party, no get-together, not even a small one. A Chinese takeaway and couple of beers was the extent of their silver wedding celebrations and they both knew they were lucky, it could be much worse.

Tess couldn't help but feel sorry for all the younger couples that had to continuously post pone their weddings. More than once she had remarked to Tim—how awful that must be and nobody would ever think this kind of thing could happen. These were really 'unprecedented times'.

So, almost a year after their anniversary, Tess and Tim settle for a barbeque with the neighbours and are happy with that. Tess still hung up silver and pink (her bridesmaids dresses colour) balloons with the numbers two and five emblazoned on them and did her best to make their back garden festive. Polly and Seán are roped into arranging the tables and chairs. It was only going to be the neighbours on either side of them that were invited, so in all it would just be three households. Tess was stressing to her children that the three tables must be a least six foot apart and that they were to keep their distance from the visitors.

Luckily, the weather was holding up and it was warm enough for them to hold it outdoors. Otherwise Tess was emphasising to a truculent Polly they would have to postpone it for another day. Polly really couldn't care less and had to stop herself from arguing back at how strict her mother was when she wouldn't allow Polly to attend any of her friends' outdoor parties.

Tess charges Polly with the job of placing mini bottles of sanitising hand gel at each guest's place setting and disappears inside to grab the cutlery, that she saves for special occasions. The barbeque is to start around two and Tess reassures herself it should be all wrapped up by six, it gets chilly by then at this time of year. Sensible and cautious is how Tess would describe her guests and they were good neighbours also. Ann and her husband Ger were on one side and the side closest to Seán's music shed but they never complained about the drumming. Seán and his band Six Cross were upping their game and practising more than ever, after another local band Minimum Wage, were starting to match their number of likes on Instagram.

Ann was gifted musically herself and a beautiful singer, she always encouraged the youngsters in their musical efforts. Peggy and John at the other side were retired and never put in on anybody. They were living in River Crescent the longest and had three grown up children they had reared there. It was just the two of them now and they understood the noise that surrounded young people and, in a way, they missed it in their own house.

River Crescent was more a keyhole shape than crescent. It was so named for the river Óir that ran behind it. It was built in the fifties and was a small estate with a total of twenty houses. Its houses were arranged around an oval shaped green that had served as a playing area for the children of now varying generations that have grown up there. Up to recent times, everybody got on very well together and maintained the green and footpaths themselves to a high standard. It was only in the last couple of months that friction had reared its head. The house directly opposed Tess and Tim Powers' home had some ladders outside it one morning. The Powers had thought nothing of it and didn't even notice the ladders were gone in the matter of an hour before any visible work had been done to the house exterior. It was only when Tess was in her back garden hanging out her washing that Peggy called over to her and with the box hedging between them filled Tess in on the latest neighbourhood gossip.

Apparently, someone in the neighbourhood had reported the ladders going up and the guards had arrived and told the window cleaners to take them down, as it was unnecessary work and against restrictions. Tess leaned in closer to hear Peggy, as was her habit when there was something juicy going on and they didn't want anyone to overhear. Both ladies forgot about their own social distancing when it suited. "In the name of God, how could you catch Covid from cleaning the outside of someone's windows, would you ever tell me, Tess?"

It is now nine o'clock and there is no shutting Tess up now, and the rest of them aren't much better. Being so starved of social interaction and company other than their own families, the six adults are now well on their way to being badly hungover tomorrow. Once Seán and his friends had their fill of burgers and sausages they had long disappeared into the music shed, they are oblivious to the raucous conversation going on in the back garden. The Six Cross members had promised Tess they would keep their social distance as they practiced.

All promises were soon forgotten once the shed door was closed and they were viewing their latest Instagram post, huddled around Seán's phone. Polly too was well distracted by her phone, until her facetime conversation with her friends

66

had to be interrupted by the call of nature. On her way back to her bedroom, she could hear her mother's voice above all others as she was about to put her earbuds back in.

Polly's bedroom is at the back of the house and overlooks the barbeque area, that is now strewn with empty wine and beer bottles. The bottles of hand sanitiser disregarded in favour for bottles of beer and cider. It's a stuffy night and Polly has her bedroom window open and is about to close it to block out the rowdy adults below. Just as she is reaching towards the window handle her attention is grabbed by the mention of her godmother's name, Jenny.

"I mean, Peter is nice and everything, and it's great that she has managed to meet someone at this stage of her life. She's no spring chicken after all. It's what she's marrying into that what's worrying me." Tess is speaking so fast now it's hard to keep up, and in answer to her guests' quizzical looks, she obligingly goes on to fill in the blanks for them. "It's that Paul, what's his name, Lombard, you remember he was in the paper for stalking his ex-girlfriend, he even broke into her house last year, I think it was around St Patrick's Day."

To this Polly could hear a collective sharp intake of breath from Tess's audience, encouraged by this Tess goes on to explain that Peter's sister, Clara is married to this monster. To the enjoyment of the others, Tess goes on in what she thinks is a lower tone to say they even think he might know more about poor Tim's mother disappearing decades ago. He's been heard shouting about it when he's full of drink, you know. I think he's working as night watchman up the Ardview Hotel now, imagine the come down for him, he used to be a detective before all this happened.

If Tim were less drunk, he may have been offended or at least annoyed by Tess using his sister's future marriage and his mother's disappearance for solacious conversation, but he was reclining back in one of the sun loungers, mellowed by the alcohol in his system and was happy for his wife to do all the entertaining. It meant he could relax, but couldn't help chipping in, "maybe all these lockdowns and wedding postponements are a sign from the universe—maybe it's not meant to be."

Everyone else laughed at this, everyone except Polly.

It's almost midnight by the time the revellers leave, it had gotten too cold outside, and they had moved indoors for the final couple of hours. All social distancing rules well forgotten with the hugs and the kisses that were exchanged in the front porch. With the strains of "we must do this more often", ringing in her ears, Polly finally gets to sleep.

Even though Polly hasn't indulged like her parents the night before, she still feels shattered and her head is aching. Standing at the kitchen sink, she sips on water to wash down the two painkillers she has just taken. The overheard conversation from the barbeque below her window has left her unsettled and she has a lot of questions to ask her parents. It was never really spoken about openly on her father's side of the family and Polly feels resentful that she had to hear the truth about her grandmother second hand.

Last night, she wasn't deliberately eavesdropping and is half sorry now that she heard anything, but she can't unhear it now. When her parents eventually groggily shuffle down the stairs into the kitchen, she loudly and deliberately chastises them for being hypocrites and doing all the things they forbade her from doing. They both just look at her sheepishly until her mother breaks the silence with "not now, Polly, give us a break," before retrieving the painkillers from Polly's hand.

Polly decides this isn't the time to quiz them on family history and storms out of the kitchen with a reproachful and disappointed stare in her mother's direction. Who needs them anyway, she can find out what she needs to know on the internet.

It didn't take Polly long to find out what she needed online, and it was the topic of conversation in the group chat with her friends that morning. The thought of Paul Lombard still being free and working so near the gang of friends drew gasps from her teenage peers. Lucy, one of the more dramatic in the group, exclaims, "We could be murdered in our beds, and to think we were up around that old hotel, and he is working there!"

The girls regularly met up with some of the local boys and had been easily able to negotiate the steep cliff face that led up to the hotel by day, at night emboldened by the cover of darkness they were brave enough to walk up the long and winding driveway, as the two-night security guards didn't seem to bother patrolling the place. Boredom had made them more brazen lately and they had even gotten into the hotel, while the dozy security guards were on night duty. Lucy might think Paul Lombard was reason enough to stop hanging around the crumbling hotel and its vast grounds, but Polly thinks it the reason why they should.

Chapter 12
Late Summer 2021
Don't Let Your Guard Down

There're always too many bloody people about, Paul is deep in this thought and his brow is furrowed, but no one would know as his head is bowed down and he is keeping his face mask on all the time, he is out on one of his scouting trips. Paul is not worried about catching Covid, the mask serves him well as a deterrent to being recognised. After much consideration Paul has decided that cyclists are least likely to be stopped by garda checkpoints dotted around Waterport and all the cycling gear is good coverage. The last thing he wants is to be spotted anywhere near Emma. For the last couple of weeks, he has been keeping Emma under surveillance from as far away as possible.

Paul has systematically made a point of cycling down Emma's Street a few times a day to determine if there is any kind of pattern to her daily routine. After a couple of weeks of this, he has managed to spot her loading up her boot a couple of times with art supplies and what looks like a small cooler bag, with what he presumes to be food. Not having to be a detective, let alone a disgraced one Paul figures out that she must be planning to be away from the house for a few hours at least.

Paul knows Emma long enough to guess she's not too worried about breaking the rules about travelling unnecessarily and he has a good idea of where she would head for with her art gear in tow. Standing well back, behind one of the old chestnut trees that line the street opposite, he is well obscured by his cycling helmet and face mask, he takes note of the direction her car takes when it reaches the junction at the end of the road—and it confirms what he has already figured out.

Feeling unprepared for the task ahead Paul decides this is not the day to try and cycle to Gull Cove, and given the settled weather he knows Emma will going there again. Emma favoured sketching in the early morning before the beach gets too crowded and the morning light is gone.

The next time, he will be more organised, the next time he'll be there ahead of her, ready and waiting.

Clara and himself are so disconnected from each other's lives, she didn't even notice he has started cycling again. It only became apparent when she went out to the shed that sits at the end of their long back garden and she noticed the bike had been cleaned up and the chain was well oiled. Paul hadn't used in years; she was happy to see him taking it up again. Anything that would get him out of the house was good as far as she was concerned.

The rules keep changing all the time and Clara is beyond caring anymore. Sick of being alone, she has just seen Jenny and Peter off at the front door. They had offered to wear masks when she had invited them around for their dinner, but she dismissed it and said she would take her chances.

Growing increasingly frustrated, she feels exasperated by the stalemate she has found herself in, sharing a house with a man that she is slowly beginning to hate. It wasn't in her nature to hold so much resentment inside and she is starting to harbour dark thoughts about Paul.

Sometimes she indulges in the fantasy of Paul being gone out of her life forever, sometimes she finds herself thinking of crime programmes where so often the spouse is the murderer—she can understand it. Instead, she would be happy for Paul to just leave Waterport forever. Never having children together could mean it would be a clean break for both of them. Clara knows Paul's life would have to become very difficult for him before he would leave though.

By the time her visitors are gone, Clara is exhausted from keeping up the pretence of being happy. Not wanting to burden her brother Peter, she has been wearing a fake smile for most of the evening. Being so out of practice with entertaining or even being around people is more tiring than she remembers—having grown so used to just her own company. Clearing the dishes from the table, she wonders will the world ever be the same again.

As the full moon rises in the sky that night and is reflected on the shiny slates of her grand home, Clara is lying in her bed below reflecting on her own future and how she could be free of Paul.

Meanwhile, Paul is in the Ardview Hotel planning what he considers to be the perfect crime. Keeping a close eye on the weather forecasts he will time it just right. The weather is the most important indicator as to when Emma's art trips are planned. Early morning is the time of the day he's most likely to find her alone at Gull Cove and he knows it will have to be a fine morning too.

With daylight getting slightly later by the day, Paul will bring his bike to work with him every evening in the boot of his car. While Tommy is asleep, he will cycle to Gull Cove at around five in the morning, after watching Emma for the last few weeks he has figured out she usually leaves home around six, and he'll be there ahead of her. Tommy is a heavy sleeper and will be probably be still asleep when Paul plans to be back before their shift finishes at eight o'clock. Paul just has to hope there won't be any snoopy guards manning the checkpoints at that hour of the morning. The Ardview Hotel is nearer to Gull Cove than his house and he has done a practice run a few times, he usually takes a half hour each way, he would love to be able to boast to Tommy about his fitness, but resists.

All the boxes are ticked as far as Paul is concerned; he has the perfect alibi in the sleeping Tommy. If Tommy is questioned about Paul's whereabouts on the night in question, he's not going to admit to sleeping on the job. Paul knows Tommy will vouch for him.

The plan worked in part. Paul was right Tommy was still asleep when he got back sweaty and annoyed to the hotel from his attempt to get to Gull Cove. A good old-fashioned puncture put paid to his plans on his way to Gull Cove and he had to half walk, half run to be back in time. Pushing the bike at the same time was proving difficult so Paul ditched it in an outbuilding of an abandoned farmhouse and sprinted the rest of the way back.

When Tommy comes across him in the male changing rooms of the old leisure centre, Paul is coming out of the shower. There is no hot water supply anymore, just cold and Paul is shivering as he is drying himself off. In answer to Tommy's confused look, Paul easily lies, claiming he had been chasing off some teenagers that had been hanging around outside. With a shrug of his shoulders Tommy accepts this and strolls back to his coffee flask at the front desk.

Paul didn't want to attempt this plan again; it was too risky and resigns himself to come up with a new one. Maybe he would wait until autumn, the encroaching darkness would be to his advantage, there might be more freedom of movement and less garda checkpoints if the restrictions are eased by then. The thought of bumping into his former colleagues, Brown and Doyle, made him sick.

Chapter 13
Early Autumn 2021
Close Contact

Rosie knew Emma was hard, but it wasn't until this pandemic did she realise how hard her daughter really was. Emma astounded her mother with her complete lack of empathy for people that were really suffering. They had been watching the main evening news together one evening and it had shown clips of the desperate hospital cases in Italy and the high death rate, when Emma mumbled they were all old anyway, a shocked Rosie turned and stared at her.

Emma had a hard look in her eyes and was unrepentant. Not for the first time Rosie wondered how her own flesh and blood could look at the world in such a cold way and remain oblivious to how selfish she sounded. On her less charitable days Rosie wondered if Emma's adoptive mother Mary O'Brien had something to do with it. Rosie knows she, herself was no innocent when she had an affair with Mary's husband decades ago and knows she bears some responsibility for bringing Emma into the world. With no help from her own parents, Rosie had been forced into putting Emma up for adoption. Consoling herself that she had done her best, and was relieved when she eventually heard Emma had been adopted by her biological father, Tom O'Brien, unknown to his wife Mary and Emma had been raised with an older half-sister Essie. Rosie contemplates if Emma was just born this way.

If Emma was tough on the world around her, she was brutally harsh about her adoptive mother. On many occasions, Rosie had to remind Emma not to speak ill of the dead—when Emma would refer to some hurt from her childhood, that she inevitably blamed on alcoholic Mary. When Rosie reminded her once that being an alcoholic was a disease, Emma retort was to blame Rosie for her shabby upbringing. Rosie will never forget the words that stabbed like a knife, "You're as much to blame, the affair you had with my father drove her to drink."

If Rosie was a braver woman, she might have told Emma her father was no bystander in all this. But Emma seemed to gloss over her father's responsibility, but virtue of dying he seemed to be exonerated. But Rosie was depending on Emma now more than ever, and this made her feel very vulnerable.

It's three days since Rosie has heard from Emma and she is beginning to worry. As well as needing groceries, Rosie is also running out of her blood pressure tablets and needs Emma to collect a new prescription from the chemist. Emma also collects Rosie's pension for her too. Not being a texter, Rosie has rung Emma multiple times and decides this is just another one of her sulks.

The last day Emma was over, she was angry about her new book release. Emma had wanted a lavish book launch, but restrictions didn't allow for it and she was bitterly disappointed. When a secretly relieved Rosie tried to comfort her by saying it was probably for the best, as she wouldn't want to be responsible for a fresh outbreak of Covid, Emma exploded, "You're probably delighted, you never wanted me to publish it anyway, Covid is a handy excuse alright, a most convenient pandemic!"

Rosie would like to say that Emma was wrong about how she felt with regard to the new book, but she knew she couldn't carry the lie. Remembering Emma's anger, Rosie decides to leave it for another few days before reaching out again and picks up her phone to the local supermarket and places her order. Feeling liberated, she phones the chemist to see if anyone could deliver the prescription for her. Rosie likes the feeling of being independent of Emma and vows not to depend on her too much in the future.

"What's that smell?" Tommy is in the main function room of the Ardview Hotel and is sniffing the air around him like a bloodhound. Paul is trailing behind him, they are supposed to be fixing the large sheet of plywood that has become loose from the large panes of glass that surround the room.

"This isn't really our job, you know," Paul tells a distracted Tommy who is gazing up at the ceiling with his mouth open. Tommy is not listening to him and just points up at large reddish-brown stain on one of the false ceiling tiles directly above their heads.

Dismissing it as probably an old pipe leaking rusty water, Paul draws Tommy's attention away from it and offers to go pick up a takeaway, his 'treat', he reassures a hungry Tommy. "Well, I suppose the pipework has never been replaced since the place was built in the seventies, dampness could explain the smell too," agrees a placated Tommy. While Paul is gone into town to the chip shop, Tommy might have seen the small group of teenagers that were crossing the carpark towards his car with a can of aerosol, but Tommy never really bothered to watch the security camera monitors, not when there was something decent to watch on his laptop.

Chapter 14
Living with Covid
Late September 2021

"I don't care what you say, it's an accident waiting to happen!"

By now, the pubs have reopened and Matty and Bobby are back in their rightful place sitting at the bar in Ryan's. When the two men had reclaimed their seats after such a long absence, they had felt a bit brazen, but after a couple of pints they were back to their usual business of putting the world to rights. Bobby has embraced the new "European way of doing things, most cities in Europe have the outdoor dining thing going on," as he calls it.

To which Matty gives a sniff and says, "We might as well be still under British rule, we were only under one master then, isn't that right, Rosie?"

Rosie is behind the bar wiping down the mahogany bar top with a distracted look on her face. Not having the energy to get involved in another of their debates, Rosie says nothing and busies herself stocking the shelves. They are discussing the newly established shared space in the city centre, that allows vehicles and pedestrians equal access to the narrow streets, and this combined with outdoor dining furniture has Matty fired up.

After all the intermittent pub closures, Rosie has lost some of her staff to more secure jobs and to be honest she can't blame them. Between organising outdoor seating, mask wearing and checking customers Covid certs she was worn out. Emma sulking and doing a disappearing act wasn't helping either. If she heard one more politician on the news talking about 'wet pubs', she would scream; she hated the term and really feels some of those in charge are so far removed from running a business, they might as well be on the moon.

Rosie is so tired, she is even considering offering Matty a few hours casual work behind the bar, he seems to have plenty of time on his hands. Of course, she will have to run this by Emma first, if she ever catches up with her. To cheer herself up, Rosie rings her longstanding hairdresser, hoping to get an appointment before the weekend. After being told that she would be put on a waiting list and would probably get one in about three weeks, Rosie hangs up glumly and wonders what the world has come too. Rosie knows a few of her friends had been still getting their hair done on the quiet with their own hairdressers, she regrets now playing by the rules.

"How did I know it was the wrong car?" Alex hisses at Polly.

The small group of teenagers are huddled behind a skip at the far end of the Ardview carpark and Polly is beginning to regret her retelling of the Paul Lombard story to her friends, she also regretting getting Alex involved. Everybody knew he had a crush on her and would do anything she asked of him. Feeling guilty now for taking advantage of that, she's also worried that he may think she owes him something now. At least they were all wearing those Covid facemasks, but for the avoidance of detection rather than Covid.

Upon his return, Paul doesn't notice the teenagers and their handiwork, such is his hurry to enjoy his takeaway. Crouching down and trying to keep a low profile was giving Polly a pain in her back and her legs were starting to stiffen. They had just witnessed Paul Lombard pull back into the carpark with a brown paper bag that was steaming with the aroma of vinegar, they could even smell it from their distance away. Hunger was added to the list of discomforts the youngsters were feeling and they decided to make a run for it once Paul had disappeared inside. Having cleared the carpark in a matter seconds, they scrambled down the rough grass of the cliff side easily and were on the footpath that was headed to the chipper.

Only after they had consumed their greasy takeaway on one of the picnic benches on the green opposite the small shopping complex, Polly reprimands her friends. The others just look at their feet and slowly a small giggle turns into belly laughs as they think about their own stupidity. Alex had sprayed the word KILLER on the bonnet of the wrong car and even though they were worried about some of the car park security cameras that may be still working, they assure each other their masks and hoodies hid their identities and they were right.

After Polly had done her research after overhearing her drunken parents' conversation at the barbeque, she had decided this man Paul was responsible for her late grandmother's disappearance or murder and she and her friends were going to make him suffer. After all, the adults were doing nothing about it and besides it would give the gang something to do—they were so bored. Unknown to her parents, Polly and her friends had been hanging about on the grounds of the hotel and collecting all sorts of rubbish from the old storage sheds and glass houses and having small bonfires on what used to be the golf course.

Lately though, this had grown tedious, and they had been venturing so far undetected into the hotel itself late in the evenings. The plywood hoarding that was in place of the large sheet glass windows were easily dislodged and the teenagers had grown increasingly daring as time and lockdowns wore on. When Polly told her friends that there was a murderer on duty as a security man at night, it gave their trips an added edge and sense of danger.

When Paul and Tommy emerged blinking in the sunlight the next morning, they were shocked to see the message emblazoned on Tommy's car. Paul although he didn't admit it to Tommy, knew that somehow the message was meant for him. Vowing to keep his wits about him and actually do his job of monitoring the place properly in future, he settles down to a restless day of broken sleep.

Chapter 15
Wash Your Hands

Margo hasn't been sleeping well either; she has too much energy with no way of expending it. Being used to activity her mind is restless with regret as she lies down at night. People she had assumed where her friends had grown distant during the pandemic, and she has abandoned putting updates into the Neighbourhood Watch WhatsApp group. What was the point? they usually went ignored and they were only some many times you could say "Stay safe" without it becoming patronising as well as repetitive.

Even her taste in radio had changed, she has abandoned her usual Mo Dunphy show in the afternoons for a mixture of podcasts and she doesn't miss the misery and gloom that the national broadcaster dished out constantly. Even to a formerly self-righteous individual as Margo, Mo Dunphy repeatedly telling all the callers to "wash their hands" at every ad break felt condescending and downright insulting at this stage. People knew what they were supposed to be doing by now, it's time to give people credit to do the right thing.

Sick of stomping around the same neighbourhood Margo has begun to venture further afield and is enjoying the change of scene. Inter county travel was allowed again and she was going to take full advantage of it. Getting to know the bus schedule is a novelty for her and she plans days out for herself, knowing she has no one to please but herself is liberating. Having long given up hope of ever becoming part of a group of friends, she has accepted that it's time to stop trying to initiate friendships with other women, who were so set in their ways and comfortable in their own little friend groups.

Unknown to Emma, Margo has possibly saved her life a couple of times. Summer has given way to autumn and Gull Cove has become one of Margo's favourite places to visit. Without the frenzy of summer visitors, Margo finds it peaceful. Not being a driver, she takes the bus as far as the busy seaside town of Strámor and walks the short distance to Gull Cove. Emma also prefers the quieter, but still warm days of autumn to the bustle and noise of high summer, for her sketching trips to Gull Cove.

Margo may have felt invisible and not relevant to most people, but there was one man who noticed her, and she had changed his plans a couple of times. If Emma had not been so distracted by her art, she may have felt somebody watching her or even a shadow that shouldn't be there looming behind her. So, intent on catching the climb of a seagull upward, Emma has no clue that her would be murderer is close by. The narrow road that Margo is walking is behind the sandhills that Emma is perched on, as Margo moves closer in Emma's direction, she see a figure heading towards the sandhills.

At first, she's perplexed as to why he's wearing a face covering out in the open air, she herself had even given up wearing one and decides some people must still be nervous of the virus. The man's identity remains unknown to Margo, but in her usual manner of saying hello to everybody, she shouts out a cheery, "Good morning, lovely day for it."

The man doesn't answer and briefly looks startled and scurries in the direction of Strámor. Margo is left thinking how rude and that she really must be invisible. All this goes on behind Emma and she doesn't even realise that anybody is there. Deciding to go without her hearing aid that day has rendered Emma even more vulnerable than she realises. As the high winds that reach the sandhills can be quite strong, they create a shrill whining in her hearing aid, and she finds the feedback annoying and distracting. Besides, she had no intention of interacting with anyone today, not even her mother Rosie.

The second time Paul attempted to get Emma on her own at Gull Cove, he didn't even manage to get out of his car. Having psyched himself up for another attempt on Emma's life, his heart was racing and his hands were sweaty on the steering wheel. As he drove through Strámor on his way to where he expected Emma to be, he spotted Margo getting off the bus and start her short walk in the same direction. "For God's sake, that bloody woman is a nuisance, can't she get a new hobby, instead of walking the highways and byways!"

Swinging the car around aggressively at the first opportunity, Paul shifts roughly into first gear and decides he needs a drink. Even though it's only half nine in the morning, he heads back into the city to the only pub that has a docker's licence. Going into the subdued light of Gordon's quayside bar, the smell of last night's cigarette smoke greets him at the doorway, giving way to the smell of stale beer as he goes deeper into the pub's dark interior. While waiting to be served, he helps himself to some of the hand sanitiser that is on offer on the bar counter. Paul's hands are still shaking with unspent adrenaline as he is enthusiastically rubbing in the hand sanitiser, as if to rub away the morning's failings.

Chapter 16
Breaking the Rules
Early October 2021

"It's the sign of the Devil, you know!" Lucy is sitting cross-legged on Polly's bedroom floor. Polly has just shown her three long scratch marks just above her right ankle. The angry redness of the marks has been subdued by the white antiseptic cream Polly has liberally covered them with. Enjoying the dramatic reaction of her friend, Polly doesn't correct her and takes pleasure in the exaggerated gasps from Lucy.

Polly knew that Lucy loved all that sort of thing and was forever telling her about supernatural podcasts and ghost hunting programmes that Lucy loved to watch. During the second lockdown, the girls even made a Ouija board from an old pizza box that Polly had retrieved from the bin and had set it up outdoors on the glass topped garden table in the back yard. Back then, they were all more conscientious about the social distancing rules and the girls had dutifully tried to stay six feet apart, as best they could around the large square of greasy cardboard. Now they enjoyed collective eye rolls and deep sighs when anyone chastised them for hugging or being too close to each when sharing gossip.

Polly doesn't want to deflate Lucy's excitement by telling her that it's more likely she got those scratches last night when she was scrambling down the cliff face that fronted the Ardview Hotel when that creep Paul Lombard was chasing them. Usually, she would tuck her jeans into her socks to avoid this, but last night she didn't have time. They were both giggling now at how silly they were to think that podgy old fella had a chance in hell of catching them anyway. The two girls and their friends had used the cliff and the hotel grounds as their own personal playground, they had a well-worn path that led through the scrub which made the sheer cliff face much easier to negotiate.

Bored now with looking at Polly's leg, Lucy suggests they try the Ouija board, Polly agrees. Never tiring of fooling Lucy into believing the 'messages' that are coming through, Polly retrieves it from under her bed. Telling Lucy to keep her voice down, in case her parents overhear them, Polly puts on her best poker face and calls out to the 'spirit world'. The girls plan to watch something on Netflix when they are finished communicating with the other world. That should bring them right up to end of the school day, Polly will sneak back downstairs at the right time and bang the front door loudly for the benefit of her ailing parents to herald 'her return and the end of her 'school day'.

Even though it's a bit of chore having to leave meals and drinks outside their bedroom door with painkillers a few times a day, Polly is overall enjoying her parents' confinement very much. Seán and herself have an arrangement not grass each other up and are getting on better than ever, without their parent's interference. Feeling peckish and in a generous mood

Polly helps herself to her mother's debit card to order pizza, she even includes her brother's choice of pizza too.

Under normal circumstances, Tim and Tess wouldn't mind Polly having her friends over, but these weren't normal circumstances. The couple are totally at the mercy of their children for the time being—as they both have contracted Covid 19. Resting sporadically during the day and saving the heavier sleep-inducing painkillers for night has proved to be more difficult than they thought.

Bizarrely, even though they have the same virus, the symptoms are varied between them. Tess is more tired with it and Tim is feverish and has lost his sense of taste. Being stuck in the master bedroom together has made them irritable and it doesn't help that they have themselves to blame for it. The worst part is they can't even blame the kids for bringing it into the house.

When they tested positive at first, they almost made a joke of it and said it would be a great excuse to sit around watching television all day—almost like a surprise holiday. The novelty soon wore off, the constant repeats on the old small portable television that was in their bedroom were starting to drive them mad. The television was around since they first got married and they could only get four channels on it. In the afternoons, there were low budget made for television films with predictable endings and quiz shows with incessant advertisements in between for stairlifts and funeral packages.

"That'll tell you who these programmes are aimed at— it's bloody depressing!"

Tess agrees with her husband and with a nod turns on her side and pretends to be asleep until she is. The television programmes are not the only thing on repeat around her. Tess knows deep down even though Tim hasn't come out and said it yet, he really blames her for their situation. After the success of their summer barbeque, Tess had gotten a taste for entertaining and being around people again. Instead of just inviting his sister Jenny and her fiancé Peter around for a meal over the weekend, she had invited her own siblings and their families too. Tim had said they were asking for trouble and Tess had dismissed him with a wave of her hand. Since then, at least three of their guests had tested positive.

Tess knew eventually Tim would be telling her 'I told you so'. The couple are grateful now that they had decided to convert their walk-in wardrobe into an ensuite a few years ago, at least they got something right.

Covid-19 wasn't the only reason Tess was feeling lousy, the night before she had tested positive, she had snatched Polly's phone from the dining room table while Tess had gone to the bathroom. Despite repeatedly telling Polly later that evening that she hadn't seen it, Tess knew exactly where it was. It was in the back pocket of her jeans and as soon as she got a chance, she slipped it behind the cushions on the large sofa in the sitting room. Tess had long figured out the pin on Polly's phone and had on occasion surreptitiously sneaked a look at the text messages her daughter received and sent.

Having noticed Polly swiping the four-digit code when she was sitting on the sofa behind her, pretending to watch the television and Polly was sitting on the rug in front of the fire directly in front of her. Tess's eyesight couldn't stretch to reading the messaging that was going on that evening, she had managed to notice, however, the swift Z movement of Polly's index finger and Tess rightly figured out the code was 1379.

It seemed a bit random to Tess and figured it was just easy to remember because it was the four corner numbers of the keypad. After Tess had retreated to her own bedroom and read the messages, she had reassured Polly that "...the phone would turn up and did she check behind the cushions on the sofa, it might have fallen out of your pocket, like it did the last time, remember?"

After reading the message thread on her daughter's phone, Tess feels a mixture of relief and confusion. The smell on Polly's clothes is as she suspected from being around bonfires—a smell that Tess had rightly associated with Halloweens from the past and her own childhood, at least they weren't setting fire to private property. Most of the messages were fairly innocent. The more recent messages are alluding to some place called 'The Wreck', and some fella the kids refer to as 'Killer'. Tess doesn't like the sound of this and assumes it must be some nightclub that let in underage kids and 'Killer', must be a nickname for some new friend that has joined the gang. The trouble is she can't ask Polly, and this is the most frustrating part of it.

While Tess is sleeping, Tim is trying to connect to Netflix and is not having much success. When he finally chooses something to watch, the screen freezes. A message pops up in the sidebar telling him there are too many users. Tim doesn't understand why this is happening, he thought he heard the front door slam this morning as Polly left for school, or was that yesterday morning? That should be Polly accounted for, and the constant drumbeat coming from the garden shed gives Seán's location away. Even though Seán is supposed to at college, assuming the reason to be more free lectures, he hasn't the energy to worry about why he's home so early in the afternoon.

Feeling utterly miserable, his current situation reminds him of childhood holidays stuck in a pokey caravan while it's raining for a week, with his equally unhappy siblings. As a last resort, Tim finds an old paperback that has lain unread on his bedside locker for ages and reintroduces himself to the written word.

Even though it's early October and there is a nip in the air, Margo has kept up her regime of getting out into the fresh air as much as possible. Over the last couple of months, she has found it be uplifting and has given her a renewed energy for life. A life, however, different to her pre-pandemic one and that is not necessarily a bad thing. With people out and about and mixing a bit more now, she has bumped into a couple of the old Neighbourhood Watch members and been asked about when the meetings will be starting again. What Margo would like to say is that she's really not bothered with people that aren't really her friends and that they can run their own meetings in future! What she does tell them is that she is no longer interested, and she has done her bit.

Margo's husband Jack has noticed a positive change in her also. No longer obsessed with organising meetings and running around for everybody else, she seems less stressed and easier to be around. Not really sure what Margo gets out of her long hikes in the fresh air, it wouldn't be his scene, he's happy that she's happy. Jack regrets now he may have been a bit neglectful of his wife with all the long hours he works as a plumber and has made a point of spending more time with her. They are in a good place, so when she rings him out of the blue in the middle of a workday, Jack is half expecting an invite to meet up for lunch when he sees her name flash up on his phone.

Jack is at his wife's side within a half an hour, and they are both staring down at a pathetic little black and white kitten that is curled up in a ball in Margo's large Tupperware container. Jack is rubbing his stubbled chin, wondering how he ended up in a derelict shed surrounded by curious cattle and why there is a very expensive looking man's bike amongst all the rusty and obsolete farm tools that look like they haven't been used in decades. All that is left of the original farmhouse across what would have once been a farmyard is the crumbling four corners that the cattle are using as scratching posts now. It was a common enough setup, for the original farmhouse to be left to nature's devices, when the older family members die, the younger ones usually built a new bungalow or two storey houses if planning permission allowed, somewhere else on the farm property.

Jack is pondering on this and feels a bit melancholy about the old homesteads that may have witnessed the Great Famine and God knows what else, being neglected and written off. "If these walls could talk, eh?" he mutters softly to Margo, but more so to himself.

"Did you hear me?" Margo is staring up at her husband now, with a hopeful expression on her face. "Do you think he or she, I can't really tell, is a stray?"

Jack reassures her that looking at the state of the poor creature, definitely nobody is looking after him or her and before she even asks, Jack can read the question in her eyes and answers her before she speaks. "Of course, we can bring little Jess home, I have some clean rags in the van, we'll wrap the poor kitten up well for the journey home." In answer to his wife's raised eyebrow, Jack declares, "Sure we'd have to call him after Postman Pat's cat, he's the image of him!"

When they had Jess well wrapped up and fast asleep in his Tupperware bed in the passenger footwell of the van, Margo hesitated before getting into the passenger seat. Jack followed Margo's stare in the direction of the shed that had been Jess's home, before Margo had heard the faint meowling from that direction. Margo had been picking blackberries with great plans for recipes she had seen online, banana bread was so last year she had joked earlier that morning to Jack, before heading off to catch the bus to Strámor. Jack would have happily dropped her off before he went to work, but Margo enjoyed the bus trip and had turned into a bit of a people watcher. It was part of the day out for her now, and she valued her little bit of independence.

On catching sight of the sickly thin kitten, Margo instinctively tossed the blackberries from the Tupperware container and fished the animal out from between the shiny spokes of what had been Paul Lombard's bike. At first she hadn't paid much attention to how out of place such a well maintained and what she had perceived to be expensive bike was doing amongst all the relics of well past farming days. It was while she was waiting for Jack to turn up, an idea struck her. It would give her independence and keep her fit—if she was more religious woman, she would see it as a sign from God. The fact it was a man's bike didn't bother her, she was a tall, long-legged woman and the crossbar wouldn't be a problem for her.

Jack had to hand it to Margo, she did put up a good case. It was true, the bike may have been stolen and they would give a full description and photographs to the guards, and it

94

might make its way back to its rightful owner. It was really the right thing to do. Even so, Jack couldn't help feeling guilty and kept looking around as he loaded the bicycle into the back of his van. A criminal he could never be, as his wife had to keep reassuring him that they were doing nothing wrong.

By the time Jack and Margo had gone to the guards with all the information on the bike, Jess was well settled in and proved to be a quiet little companion for Margo. Having given the bike a good clean, it had been a bit muddy—Jack was sure it wasn't in that shed for long, a few months at most, as there wasn't any rust just in need of a puncture repair. Leaving photographs and their contact details with the guards, they regretted there didn't seem to be any security serial number on the bike—they felt there was no more they could do just wait.

The guard on the desk that day when Margo and Jack had called into the station thought it was strange that a bike this valuable didn't have a serial number. Unknown to him though there had once been a serial number on it, but Paul Lombard had scraped it off when he took it from the stolen property unit at the back of the barracks, a few years back.

That bike proved to be well used by Margo; she never knew she was enjoying the spoils of crime.

Chapter 17
An Abundance of Caution
Mid-October 2021

"Are you sure you've checked everywhere?" Lucy asks Polly for the third time.

Polly's answer comes in an aggravated hiss, "Yes, I've told you already, the only place it can be is up in the wreck!" As they now called the Ardview for short.

The two girls exchange worried glances, as they really don't want to go back up there again. After last night's close call, they had decided to stop pushing their luck and stay away from the place. It had just been the two of them last night, Lucy was anxious to get some footage on her phone of the old place. After watching paranormal programmes that had caught footage of spirits, Lucy wanted to try it for herself and had begged Polly to go with her. The rest of their friends had opted out as it was a school night and their parents had begun to home in their teenagers' nocturnal activities, it was after all the first term of their Leaving Cert year.

Lucy had lied to her parents about studying with Polly and the two girls began their familiar trek. Polly's parents though out of quarantine were still not fully back to full health, and she had heard them moaning to each other in the kitchen about having Long Covid. Telling them that she had to go over to Lucy's to collect some schoolbook that she had loaned her, her parents barely raise a goodbye and 'don't be late back' to her figure disappearing out the front door.

Lucy is fired up with enthusiasm as they climb the steep hill and reassures Polly, "We've a better chance of catching something when it's only the two of us."

Polly replies sarcastically, "But it's not just the two of us, is it? Those two so-called security guards will be here too."

"Ah those two dopes, don't mind them; they couldn't catch a cold, but that Paul fella does give me the creeps alright. It's probably part of being an empath, it's a blessing and a curse, I sense things."

Polly laughed at Lucy's high opinion of herself, but warned Lucy not to be too cocky, and reminded Lucy that he could be a killer.

It's almost nine o'clock by the time the girls gain access through the debris-filled ballroom. As usual, they slip easily behind the plywood sheet that has allowed them access on other visits. They must pick their steps carefully so as not to disturb any of the discarded rubbish around the floor. Although they couldn't articulate their disgust at the smell vocally, they both held their noses until they were free of the ballroom area. The wrong move could give them away as it would be impossible not to make any noise on the wooden dance floor if something were to fall over. Glad now they had worn dark clothes and soft runners they moved silently and efficiently through the building and headed across the main reception area undetected for now.

Tommy was sitting with his back to the main reception area, he had been absentmindedly swivelling in the old office chair. After a couple of months on the job, Tommy figured out this was the best spot in the building for mobile phone reception. Facetime was a new concept for him and he was looking at his wife's face on the screen of his phone, while two silent shadows fell on the wall adjacent to the stairwell that led to the first floor.

"What was that?" his wife interrupted their conversation about which tiles to pick for the kitchen floor.

"What was what?" came Tommy's confused reply, the look of concentration on her face was starting to make him nervous. By now his wife is squinting into the phone screen and all her attention is on the background area behind Tommy's right shoulder. After a few seconds of straining her eyes, she asked Tommy if someone was there with him, as she thought she saw movement in the background.

"Ah," came Tommy's relieved reply, "that's just Paul, you know the fella I told you about, the other security guard." Satisfied with this, she went back to holding samples of the different (although they all looked the same to Tommy) kitchen tiles up for his consideration.

Tommy is wrong about Paul's whereabouts, he's in the back office deeply engrossed in something on his laptop.

Paul is on the internet looking up shrews and how to get rid of them. Eventually, the opposite day shift of security had called out a pest control company to get to the bottom of the now large brownish red stain that had spread across the ceiling tiles in the ballroom and had found the decaying body of a rat. Poison had been put in traps outside a few months previously and the rodent experts figured, this one had burrowed its way into the false ceiling and had died from the poison there. More poison was put down and the bait traps were liberally spread around the building inside and out.

While the pest control company were there, they had told the day security that they had bigger problems with the shrew infestation they had found nests of them in the false ceiling, and they were very hard to get rid of. Being part of the hedgehog family, they were a protected species, and you weren't allowed to poison them. The reproduction rate of shrews was incredibly fast, and they survived on eating mice and insects. Even though these were smaller than mice, they were more vicious and insidious. Paul hated rodents more than anything and if he were to be honest about it, he had a full-blown phobia.

After scrolling through videos of mostly American hillbilly types setting traps in buckets and all sorts of complicated techniques of poisoning them (no such thing as a protected species there), Paul shut down the laptop, feeling more freaked out now than ever. Tommy couldn't understand why Paul was so bothered about it. Rumour had it that the hotel group, Drury's, were putting the place on the market and that it would be either demolished or completely gutted and turned into apartments. This was no consolation for Paul, as he knew he would be here for another few months and that was a long time to be on the lookout for shrews and rats crawling around the place. Paul needn't have worried; it wasn't going to be a problem for him much longer.

Paul didn't realise that right there and then he should have been on the lookout for two human intruders, equally insidious as the shrew population.

"I'm telling you I heard something," Polly has interrupted Lucy mid-sentence.

Lucy had put her phone on record and had been about to finish her question to the spirits. Lucy was projecting her voice around the empty bedroom that had formerly been known as the bridal suite, just as she had seen paranormal investigators do on the television. Before she got to complete her question, Polly had grabbed her arm and hissed shush to her, before giving Lucy the gesture of pressing her index finger to her lips. That was all Lucy needed to know and when she sat quietly for a minute, she heard it too.

The pair had settled themselves on top of the fourposter bed that was the centrepiece of the room. The walls bore the remains of what would have been the height of sophistication back in the seventies, when the Ardview was built. Deep red patches of velvet lined wallpaper still clung to the walls defiantly acting as a reminder to the former glory days of the hotel. The rest of the wallpaper was strewn around the floor in clumps of damp mulch. The rain had started to get into the building and the walls looked like they were crying in the more vulnerable parts of the building.

Between the now soggy wallpaper and the tattered remains of the once vibrant gold and red canopy of the bed lying on the floor, only patches of the thick carpet could be seen. It too carried the gold and red theme of the room; the large diamond shaped design of the carpet was a perfect reminder of the era in which it was laid. This too was damp in places, and the girls had felt the carpet squelch in places underfoot. The years of water damage and general neglect left a damp mouldy aroma in the room like most of the rest of the guest rooms on this floor.

Perching themselves on the bed, even though it was probably filthy too, seemed like a place of safety when they started their ghost hunt, but now it made them feel more vulnerable and isolated, as the noise they were hearing was coming from under the bed. At first it just sounded like a faint rustle, one that could easily be written off as if the breeze that was coming in the broken window had just disturbed some of the old wallpaper that was strewn around the floor.

But as the girls concentrated, it became more of a scratching sound, looking at each other with wide eyes they looked towards the door and with the expertise of a SWAT team, Polly counted her fingers up in front of Lucy's face and mouthed with exaggeration, ONE, TWO, THREE and with precise synchronisation they moved as one in a swift but loud race to the hotel room door and, forgetting all consequences of being discovered, took the descent down the wide staircase two steps at a time.

Tommy was on his 'sleep break' while all this was going on and remained undisturbed throughout. In fact, he was so tired, he slept through until the morning light was making long-fingered attempts to reach him on his mattress in the back office. Assuming that Paul had already knocked off early, as there wasn't much going on around here anyway, a well-rested Tommy got ready to go home, just as the day security shift clocked on. After a brief conversation with his daytime counterparts, which ended in them all agreeing that they may be out of a job soon enough, if the sale of the hotel goes through, he bade them a good day. Grateful for his good night's sleep, Tommy went home to a productive day of lifting the old tiles from his kitchen floor.

Unknown to Tommy, the most exciting night in the Ardview had gone on while he was there, but literally asleep on the job. Paul not usually bothered about random sounds and creaks in the old hotel but was on extra edge that night. The whole rodent thing had left him unsettled and there was no way he was going to sleep on an old mattress while God knew what could be crawling all over him. So, he didn't bother waking Tommy and decided to actually stay awake for his full shift. Enjoying a long drag on his 'herbal' cigarette outside the front entrance to the hotel foyer, his eyes were closed, and it was the most relaxed he had felt since his shift had started. Leaning up against the wall, he considered what his next career move would be, when this place finally was sold.

The only security cameras that were working were focused on its main entrance. With the habit of covertness built in at this stage, Paul automatically stayed out of camera range, even when he wasn't up to no good. The emphasis on monitoring only the hotel entrance, even the cameras that used to monitor random parts of the car park had been vandalised and didn't work anymore. This struck Paul as an indicator as to how little there was left to protect inside the hotel. The main priority now was to keep people out from an insurance point of view.

Nowadays, apparently even a burglar can sue the property owner if they injure themselves. Even with Paul's skewed vision of right and wrong, this seemed off to him. Eventually the coldness of the night persuaded Paul to reluctantly return to the rodent infested hotel and he was just stubbing out his smoke on the cracked footpath, when he heard the unmistakable sound of footsteps running away from the hotel.

By the time Paul rounds the corner and a blast of cold wind hits him in the face, Lucy has already started her well-practiced descent down the cliff face, he only catches sight of the second athletic looking figure, and he hesitates briefly before he decides to give chase.

Fear gives way to anger as Paul assumes the petite, longhaired girl is possibly his tormentor of recent months. The bright whiteness of the moon above lets him know that she too has long black hair, now things are starting to fit together. Why this Penny Power lookalike would be persecuting him like this has been haunting him for too long now and whatever happens he's not letting her get away with it.

Paul overestimates his own level of fitness and underestimates the sheerness of the decline when he gives chase, by the time he reaches the grass verge that marks the edge of the carpark, Paul is already winded. Driven on by his own paranoia at the sight of that long black hair following in Polly's wake, Paul abandons thoughts of his own safety and starts to run down the rough and pot holed cliff face. When Paul feels his feet are no longer under his control and are running away from him, he knows he has taken off at a too high speed, all control gone now, he begins to fall as he loses his footing.

Bracing himself for impact as he sees a large rock at the bank of the cliff hurtling towards him, just before he hits it headfirst. Bizarrely, in a split second, he grins bitterly with the irony of it, as the rock reminds him of the one Penny Power hit headfirst too, decades earlier, before he threw her unconscientious body into the sea. Unlike Penny though, Paul's head injury is fatal, no-one could have saved him now.

As Paul's body landed behind the large advertising hoarding that had served as a large camouflage to the overgrown and what proved to be dangerous cliff face—nobody found him for a full week. Tommy had turned up for work and wasn't too worried when Paul didn't turn up for his shift on the Thursday and Friday nights. Tommy didn't want to get on Paul's wrong side if he reported him missing to their employers.

It was on the Monday night, when there was still no sign of Paul that Tommy really got concerned and rang his boss Paddy to fill him in on Paul's unexplained absence. Paddy retrieved Paul's file with Clara's mobile number still listed as Paul's next of kin. After a brief chat, Clara reassured a worried Paddy that it wasn't unusual for Paul to go off by himself, and they decided to give it another day before they rang the guards. Clara had to stop herself from saying it was exactly the kind of the selfish thing Paul would do.

By the time Paul's body is eventually retrieved from its rocky hiding place, Lucy and Polly are back in the routine of school and are finally starting to focus on their Leaving Certificate exams. All plans of going back to the Ardview to look for her late grandmother Penny's bracelet are abandoned, as they concentrate on their future. With the delay in finding Paul's body, neither girl had any idea of the role they played in bringing Paul Lombard to an end.

Ironically, Lucy was convinced they had brought an evil entity on themselves that night, and in a way they had. Polly the more practically minded, thought it was a rat under the bed in that ramshackle bridal suite, making the rustling noises and it was. Both scenarios were enough to put the girls off any more nocturnal adventures. Lucy had found religion again and made a point always keeping Holy Water nearby. Even Polly had started praying to St Anthony to help her find the bracelet that was so precious to her father's side of the family.

Chapter 18
19th October 2021
Freedom Day

"Well, is it Freedom Day or not?"

Rosie is confused and is looking at Emma with her brows furrowed. Rosie had been reading the newspaper sitting at the bar before the pub opened. Today had been the day long muted to herald the lifting of all restrictions. Now it appeared the politicians were having second thoughts and Rosie feels disappointment washing over her.

"Well, it is for Paul Lombard, and definitely for his new widow!" Emma replies with a cackle. Rosie is shocked by this insensitive and inappropriate remark, especially on the day of Paul Lombard's funeral. As if this isn't bad enough, Emma goes on to point out to her horrified mother, they might actually make a few bob out of him, as the church is in walking distance of the pub. "You never know, a few of the funeral goers might end up in here."

Rosie is just glad there is no one to hear Emma in the pub, she's disgusted with her and even though she never liked Paul, she didn't like Emma's lack of respect for the dead. There was no point in even arguing with her, Rosie gave up long ago trying to teach her daughter empathy—it just couldn't be learned.

Matty and Bobby are the first customers of the day, they had been discussing Emma's book and knew to shut up about it as soon as they entered Ryan's, as it was a sore subject with Rosie. In an obvious attempt of subject change, they started talking animatedly about the weather and wasn't it a grand day for a funeral. Having mentioned the book before to Rosie and how much they had enjoyed it, they had foolishly commented on how similar the 'fictitious' town it was set in was to Waterport, to which Rosie had just given a disapproving sniff.

Matty as usual not given to picking up on social ques had even joked about how some of the characters had reminded him of people around here. Rosie not wanting to hear any more about the book, it had made her uncomfortable and knew it would draw speculation from locals, slammed down the two pints in front of Matty and Bobby and told them "this is a pub, not a bloody book club!" before snatching the money from Bobby's hand. Rosie's mood wasn't helped as earlier that day Emma announced that she would be working part-time from now on, as she had to concentrate on writing a sequel.

If Emma was hoping to benefit from Paul's funeral, she was wrong. There were so few attendees that it wouldn't have made much difference to their day's profits. Anyone passing by the small group following the coffin into the church would assume, the poor turnout was to do with restrictions relating to Covid. It wasn't, it was because of how little was thought of Paul in the community and the number of enemies that he made in his lifetime. To say there were a few people relieved about his passing would be an understatement and the brown cash filled envelopes stopped falling onto the mat of 'Second Chances', as soon as the news of his death broke.

Jenny and Peter felt bad about even thinking it, and they wouldn't say it to anyone else. But once Paul's funeral was over, they both agreed it would save a lot of weirdness at their wedding now that Paul (May God be good to him) as Jenny was always sure to add when speaking of the deceased, was gone. Peter didn't like to correct Jenny with her God reference as he was sure if all the Heaven and Hell stuff, he was taught in school was true, it wasn't God Paul was dealing with.

Even though Covid had stopped them from fixing a date up to now, Paul's death had spurred them on to get a move on. Jenny knew Peter wanted to marry her and she was happy enough to just know that, but she felt it was just Covid that had been holding them back. Clara had eventually confided in them with wanting to divorce Paul, something they had long suspected, and Peter didn't really want to rub his sister's nose in it with their wedding plans.

Added to this both Peter and Jenny didn't relish the thought of sharing their day with Paul, there would be a bad atmosphere and feared it would ruin their wedding day. Instead, fate had intervened, and this had given them the freedom to choose Valentine's Day the following year. It was to be a civil service in the Tower Bridge Hotel and now, at last, they could start planning and looking forward to it.

Chapter 19
November 2021
We're All in This Together
(Start Picking Up the Threads)

To say one person was responsible for the high level of paranoia that led to Paul's death would be a mistake. Paul had wrongly thought he had one tormentor, when in fact he had a few. They were really all in this together as the saying goes but working independently of and unknown to each other. Jenny feels ashamed and when she can bear the guilt no longer and confesses to Peter about what she feels was a terrible act in view of what had subsequently happened to Paul.

They are on the sofa together watching yet another programme as Peter refers to 'I Found the Gown Again'. Jenny knows these shows are probably staged and are thoroughly predictable—the format never seems to change. A bride of any age rocks up to the bridal boutique to choose a wedding dress and inevitably her entourage prove difficult, until they all start crying when she appears in the 'perfect' dress and all within the half hour schedule—ridiculous, but she loves to watch them to get ideas for her own 'big day' and she equally enjoys Peter's playful teasing, while he too sits glued to them!

Jenny is lying across the sofa with her bare feet resting on Peter's lap. It had been the first bitterly cold day of winter and they were sitting in front of a roaring fire, with the curtains closed against the bitter northerly wind that was battering the front windows of the house. This has become a bit of a ritual most evenings since Jenny have gone back to work in Hawes Department Store as the restrictions on non-essential retail have been lifted. Peter's hands are greasy from moisturiser that he's slathering onto Jenny's feet. Peter pretends to be disgusted with this apparent act of slavery and laughs at Jenny when she lolls back giving dramatic sighs and constantly reminding him of how hard it is to be on your feet all day.

Peter reminds her that he's also on his feet all day and having to wear heavy safety boots as well. He did have to admit though his hands were never in better condition since becoming Jenny's foot masseur as the lotion was very good for his hands too. Even though Jenny's eyes are fixed on the television, Peter notices an anxious expression of worry crossing her face. Jenny doesn't even smile at his remark about the state of the big meringue the bride on the television is wearing.

"If it means that much to you, we'll have that Glow Easy on Me song, by that Avril singer for our first dance even though it sounds more like a breakup song to me." Despite her troubled mind, Jenny bursts out laughing at this. They had been trying to pick a suitable song earlier and Peter hadn't really liked any of Jenny's suggestions. Peter oblivious to getting both the singer's name and the song title wrong and

Jenny reassures him that her low mood is nothing to do with him.

With the ice broken on the topic, it didn't take much encouragement for Jenny to open up about the hair extension that she had stuffed into Paul's jacket pocket one evening when they were visiting Clara. Feeling ashamed now at the thought of it, she's shocked when Peter starts laughing at this minor offence. "Is that all?" he asks incredulously. "It's not like you murdered somebody!"

Through sniffles, Jenny gives a reply that she knows will annoy Peter, "That's the whole problem, I know you don't think Paul was capable of it, but I still think he had something to do with my mother's disappearance and he was never brought to justice for it or even investigated. It was my pathetic attempt to make him suffer and panic. I don't know what I was hoping to achieve at worst he would be in a sweat about finding a strand of hair like my mothers, at best it might encourage him to move away from Waterport completely—if he thought someone was onto him."

Jenny was wrong about Peter's reaction, he understood where she was coming from and if he had more courage, he would have done something too, to encourage Paul on his way. Feeling he had left Clara down by not protecting her from this monster, failing his sister and their late parents. Although Peter is not fully convinced that Paul was involved in Penny's disappearance, he is sure Paul wasn't a good man and it made him uncomfortable to think his sister had been under the same roof as him for years.

In fairness, when the pandemic hit. Peter and Jenny had asked Clara to come live with them and be part of their bubble and Ginger was invited too. Clara had thanked them for their offer but insisted on staying in her own house, she explained she would have no legal claim on it if she moved out—this was all Jenny and Peter needed to hear to assess the state of Paul and Clara's marriage.

When Jenny goes on to tell Peter, that's not all she did, he braces himself. For one absurd moment, he has visions of Jenny pushing Paul off that cliff on the grounds of the Ardview Hotel. Relief washes over him when Jenny says she left a voicemail on the Ardview landline number, knowing it would get back to Paul. Feeling emboldened by the grin starting to spread across Peter's face, she is almost proud when she relays her words to him. Casting her mind back, she repeats it perfectly, she remembers the phone being answered by a man who sounded like he had just woken up.

Not being sure if Paul or his co-worker would pick up, she was ready for either scenario and had her message written down in front of her to be passed on to Paul, if it wasn't him. Although she would have preferred it to be Paul that answered, she would have liked to have heard even a shocked gasp from him. Instead, she just asked the guy on the other end to tell Paul, "Penny rang and said she was sorry to miss you, but that she'll catch up with you another time."

Peter is wide-eyed at this admission from Jenny and feels a sense of pride in her. This was a new side to his fiancée that he had never seen before. They are both laughing by the time the television bride is crying with joy over her choice of dress. Peter jokes, "I hope I never get on the wrong side of you."

Jenny feels like a weight has been lifted off her and her mind turns to all things wedding again. The dress is sorted, and she will not divulge any detail to Peter about it, but she feels accessories are fine to speak freely of—no bad luck there. Most of her outfit is sorted, the only thing she hasn't fully decided on is her 'something old, something new, something borrowed, something blue'. Well, the dress would be new, and the other three requirements would be met by her late mother's charm bracelet. "You know the one, Peter."

He just looks at Jenny blankly.

"It's the silver chunky one, with all the charms, very seventies but I think it would fit the bill. It's old, the something blue is the tiny little dolphin charm on it and it'll be borrowed. Remember, we gave it to mam's first granddaughter that was named after her, before they shortened it to Polly. I can borrow it back from her for the day—something borrowed there sorted!"

With this, Jenny can still see a look of confusion on Peter's face and reaches for her phone. First, she has to wipe her index finger clean of the moisturising lotion before she can access her photos on it. Jenny is equally liberal with it on her hands as her feet, finding the constant hand sanitising very drying and feels her hands are starting to age prematurely because of the harsh cheap brand that they are using on the shop counter all day.

While Jenny is scrolling through her photo album on her phone, Peter abruptly shouts out, "At last! That's the perfect first dance song for us." This was a choice they both agreed on and they are smiling at the photo of the beaming Polly on Jenny's phone screen complete with the charm bracelet. The picture was taken a few years back and Jenny remarks wistfully on how little Polly smiles like that anymore; teenagers, eh?

Chapter 20
Easing of Restrictions
Valentine's Day 2022

"Stop worrying about the weather." Peter is on the phone to Jenny for the third time that morning and tired of repeating himself. It would have been easier if they had just stayed in the same house the night before the wedding, but Jenny had insisted on it being 'bad luck'. Peter knew Jenny was superstitious but when it came to their wedding, it was on another level. Peter had slept well, but by the sound of it Jenny and Clara had stayed up too late and had hit the wine a bit too hard.

Opting to stay with Clara the night before the wedding was Clara's idea and Peter thought it would be a good distraction for his sister, give her new status as a widow, it was best to keep her involved and busy. In truth they could all do with a happy distraction from all the misery going on in the world today. Just getting out of pandemic mode that mad man in Russia as Matty had put it the night before in the pub decided to unleash more horrors by planning to invade Ukraine.

Peter had to work for a few hours the day before the wedding as he had to tie up some loose ends and he and a few of his friends had called into Ryan's Bar just for a couple of quiet pints. They had ended up sitting at the bar with the two older men and had enjoyed the friendly chat and banter. As always, the conversation turned to current affairs and they all nodded and agreed that it was probably just an idle threat by an egotistical bully, turning back to their pints they started slagging Peter about his choice of honeymoon destination, calling him a cheapskate. Peter took the teasing well, he was used to it, and he really didn't care where they went—a break away anywhere would be great, given how restrictive the last two years had been.

Killarney had been Jenny's choice. They had gotten fed up with all the uncertainty about international travel and neither of them fancied wearing masks on the flight anyway. People were still coming home from foreign holidays with a dose of Covid to go with their suntans. The money they would have spent on flights was now used to book a luxurious lavish spa hotel and they were both really looking forward to it— finally they would be able to relax.

Jenny is feeling far from relaxed and is in a tizzy about the state of her bridesmaid Polly's hair. Clara was Jenny's original choice of bridesmaid, although she wouldn't tell Polly this, but Clara had felt it was too soon into her widowhood to be seen dressing up and following Jenny down the aisle, it would have felt inappropriate to her. Well right now Jenny felt a blue haired bridesmaid would be more inappropriate and dreaded how the official wedding photographs would look. Polly, on the other hand was delighted with her new look and thought that Jenny would be pleased that she had gone to so much effort. Blue was the colour theme of the wedding anyway and her hair would match her dress too.

Luckily for Polly, Jenny had changed her mind about wearing the chunky seventies style charm bracelet that had been passed down to her. It would have been too cumbersome, and Jenny was afraid the charms would snag on the pale cream bell sleeves of her dress. The bracelet would have been a nuisance on the day, but it would have matched Jenny's dress perfectly for its vintage. Although it was newly made for Jenny by a local dressmaker, it was seventies in style, and it looked beautiful on her. It was a floor-length maxi-style dress, the kind of dress her mother would have worn on special occasions and as evening wear.

Jenny remembered her mother going on nights out with her father and she thought it was very glamourous, but by the time Jenny was going on nights out herself, styles had completely changed, and the glamour was lost. It would prove to be a comfortable choice for dancing at the reception later also. Going fully for the retro look, Jenny opts for a crown of baby's breath flowers on her head instead of a veil.

For something old and blue, Jenny wore one of her late mother's silver necklaces with a blue sapphire stone pendant and she borrowed a pair of drop earrings from Clara, with similar blue sapphire stones to match the necklace.

Rosie is standing at the front door of Ryan's as the wedding car, a silver limousine with blue and silver ribbons decorating its bonnet and front grille passes by. Although Rosie can understand how the romance of Valentine's Day can attract people to choosing it as a wedding date, she still has negative associations to February 14th. It's the anniversary of the death of Tom O'Brien, the only man she had loved, he was killed in a hit and run on this date decades ago. There was no-one left to think of him except herself and his daughter Emma, and Emma was so young when he died, she doesn't really remember him at all. Tom's other daughter Essie was gone also—it's almost like he never existed.

Chapter 21
Once-in-a-Hundred-Year Event
Late February 2022

Two weeks after Jenny and Peter had made their vows, Putin had fulfilled his threat to the shocked eyes of the world and invaded Ukraine. Disbelief turned to horror when the following weeks revealed just how intent he was on his purpose. Clara was one of the first to offer her home to the incoming refugees and Putin's actions were to impact her life more than anyone else in the Waterport area in the year that followed.

Being at a loss, rattling around in the large house with just Ginger the cat for company had proved to be very lonely, despite the tension and anxiety living with Paul had brought her. 'Second Chances' had become a drop-off centre for people wishing to donate clothes and toiletries for the Ukrainian people. Clara wasn't really a believer in karma, until she had seen what had happened to Paul. Even though there was a brief investigation into Paul's death, it was ruled accidental fairly quickly and Clara thought this was a measure of disinterest by Paul's ex-colleagues. Feeling sure that it was looked upon as Paul living by the sword and dying by it—it was well known in the ranks that Paul had been mixing with drug dealers and was not one of the good guys and not just in his working hours.

Despite rationalising all this over and over in her mind, Clara feels responsible in part at least for adding to Paul's miserable last few months. Early on in the lockdown, Clara had discovered the brown envelopes on the inside mat of 'Second Chances'. It had become her habit to call into the shop every so often, they had problems with the old pipework randomly springing leaks in the past—and it was a shock to see Paul's name on all the envelopes. Knowing instantly from experience of her husband, that Paul was up to no good—she decided to leave them undisturbed.

For one so devious as Paul, Clara wondered how he could be so stupid to think that she would never call into the shop—it was after all her responsibility. Deciding to match her husband on his level of sneakiness she vowed to use his latest violation of her shop against him. Hoping, just like her new sister-in-law, Jenny that a couple of nudges might prod him into leaving Waterport for good. Having only intended on sending him one note originally, with the ominous cut-out letters from the newspaper.

When this didn't seem to do the trick, she went further with the handwritten letter that Peter had found at Second Chances. Clara had disguised her handwriting by being overly flamboyant with the ornateness of the thatched cursive and exaggerated capital letters. The reason why Paul had found the fragrance on the envelope familiar was because it was one of his wife's favourite perfumes. Clara had unintentionally handled it, after she had sprayed it liberally over her wrists and it had transferred onto the pretty writing paper when she was writing the note.

Feeling foolish now, she had confided in Jenny after too much wine, the night before the wedding—hearing it out loud had made her feel vindictive and cruel to plan something so cold-bloodedly. Throughout her confession Clara had kept her eyes on the floor, she didn't want to see a look of shock or revulsion on Jenny's face that might stop her from telling the whole story. When Clara had unloaded her nefarious behaviour onto a drunken Jenny, she looked over at her sheepishly to gauge her reaction.

Even though Jenny was sitting upright in the large cream armchair, her chin was dropped, and her eyes were closed, the wine glass was balancing precariously on the wide armrest. With a gentle tap on her shoulder, Clara roused her, and all Jenny could manage was a slurred, "What were you saying?"

Clara didn't know whether to be relieved or annoyed and ushered a swaying Jenny towards the spare bedroom that was waiting for her and that temporarily resembled a bridal boutique.

In the unfolding months, Clara had taken in Ukrainian refugees and her home was soon bustling with foreign accents and the belongings of strangers. From time to time she wondered what Paul would have made of his precious house being used in such a manner, and the thought of it made her smile—she knew he would disapprove. Clara felt she was paying a small debt to the universe for her cruelty to Paul before he died and hoped the balance would somehow tip back in her favour. The first refugee that came to stay with Clara, was also a widow named Kristina and in the fullness of time, she was to become a permanent resident.

At first, Clara had found her to be abrupt and it took months to realise Clara was mistaking Kristina's manner for rudeness when in fact it was due to the language barrier. Clara had to admit, if it was the other way around, she wouldn't be able to manage a word of Kristina's native tongue. The first conversation they had was a misunderstanding. The wardrobe in Kristina's small back bedroom had never really been used by anybody before. Clara had restored it during lockdown and was very pleased with her efforts. It was a single inlaid mahogany wardrobe and she had treated the interior of large deep drawer that was on the base of the wardrobe with beeswax.

At first Clara thought Kristina wanted to give her a bright cornflower blue jumper that Clara had admired; it was a handknit with beautiful embroidered flowers on the sleeves. One morning, Kristina had come out onto the landing holding out the jumper to Clara. Perplexed by this, Clara had thought Kristina was offering her the jumper and was trying to communicate a polite 'no thank you'. Only after Kristina persistently holding the jumper out to Clara with a sniffing noise did she take a deep inhale and realise the problem.

Nodding her head in a show of understanding, Clara had to agree alright the smell of the beeswax was a bit overpowering. Slowly, over the following months, Kristina began to master the English language and conversation became easier between them—they had a lot in common.

As the conflict in Ukraine unfolded, Clara was experiencing her own inner conflict and was torn between her head and her heart. It made absolutely no sense to her that she could spend all day with someone and not need her own space. Even in the so-called honeymoon period of her early days of marriage to Paul, she always needed a little headspace. Despite living with Kristina and bringing her in to help in 'Second Chances' most days—she didn't feel the need to get away, and it slowly crept over her that Kristina meant a lot more to her than the other refugees or anyone else in her life for that matter. Kristina's dark brown eyes were so troubled and hard to read when she first arrived in Waterport, Clara wondered what those eyes had witnessed and as they spent more time together, Kristina stopped hiding behind her long dark fringe and confided in Clara all that she had been through. Now, those dark eyes lit up whenever Clara walked into the room.

If you had said to Clara a year earlier that her life would change so dramatically in a short space of time, she would have thought you were mad. Never mind a once-in-a-hundred-year event, falling in love again would have seemed more like a once-in-a-million-year event. Clara didn't need to tell Peter and Jenny about her new relationship status, as they had sensed a connection between the two women. Nobody was more surprised than Clara herself at this new chapter in her life, she had never been drawn to women, just this one. Feeling confused by her feelings, she confided in Peter, who reassured her, "they would be happy for you, just as we are", when she wondered what her late parents would have made of it.

"Life's strange alright," Peter adds as he pulls a tarnished charm bracelet from his jeans pocket and holds it up for his sister to examine.

Clara, wondering why Peter would have such a thing in his work jeans, advises him to get it cleaned before gifting it to Jenny. He really confuses her when he adds, "Why would

I do that, she already owned it before passing it on to her niece Penny, now therein lies a mystery," he says with all the flourish of a magician when producing a rabbit from a top hat.

Not bearing it any longer, Clara playfully demands Peter to spill the beans, as she knows that what he's going to do anyway and he's just enjoying the build-up. "Fair enough; anyway, I have a feeling I better tell you before Jenny gets home, I'd say she'll kill Polly over it if she finds out."

In what turned out to a long and winding story, Clara eventually gets to the bottom of it. On first sight she had thought it was a bit gaudy and a relic from the seventies. Glad now she didn't say it as it turned out to be Jenny's late mother's and had been of great sentimental value to her.

Peter had been up the Ardview Hotel measuring up for new doorways with the other carpenters that had been contracted to work on the remodelling, on the building site that it had now become. After having a mug of tea in one of the workers portacabins, the site foreman had been telling Peter about all the stuff they had found when they were pulling the place apart. There was a large cardboard box on the plastic table next to the bits and pieces needed for the tea breaks various half eaten packets of biscuits, a half carton of milk and an assortment of different coloured Tupperware with the contents of the workers' lunches.

Encouraged by the site foreman to have a look, telling Peter, "If there's anything you fancy, you can have it, but it looks like a lot of tat to me."

Peter had thought the same, in amongst the small hotel room Bibles, Peter felt a bit weird about the Bibles being thrown out as rubbish and was just about to say it, when he spotted something familiar in amongst the detritus. Among the clunky seventies style ashtrays and odd cufflinks that had once been the height of fashion for men, was the charm bracelet that Jenny was considering wearing for her wedding day.

The site foreman raised an eyebrow, when he saw what Peter had chosen from the box of 'treasures' and laughed when Peter said his wife Jenny would be delighted. It doesn't take long for Peter to figure out that Polly must have been part of one of the teenager gangs that had been hanging around the hotel, before the building work had begun. Peter's first instinct was to tell Jenny the whole story of how he had come by the bracelet, but after talking to his sister and asking her opinion he has second thoughts. For the sake of family harmony, Clara and Peter, decide to not say anything to Jenny about it and just slip it back to Polly discreetly and Peter does.

A guilty looking Polly blushes when Peter presses it into her hand the following week when they are alone briefly in the kitchen, while Polly is visiting them and Jenny is in the bathroom.

After thanking Peter in a whisper, Polly stuffs the bracelet into her pocket and promises to take better care of it in future, and she does.

Later that evening, with the new spring stretch in the daylight, as Peter is wiping down the draining board and Jenny is upstairs in the bath, he spots an attentive little robin perched on the bird table, pecking at what was left of that morning's breadcrumbs and Peter gives a little shudder when he thinks back to almost a year ago.

Peter and Jenny are sitting at the breakfast table. It's a beautiful spring Sunday morning and they are enjoying a leisurely fry-up, as they don't have to be anywhere that day.

Jenny had been relaying another strange dream to him (she had given up calling them premonitions as Peter usually laughed at her for this). Jenny had gone into great detail and Peter can make no sense of it either. Jenny is as confused about dreaming of Clara getting married for a second time as he is. Peter has to admire Jenny's eye for detail even while she's dreaming.

Describing Clara's dress as a long straight cream lace gown with a slight train and raw silk covered cream shoes that are just peeping out from under the dress hem, to reveal dainty ivory coloured buttons along their sides. But the most bizarre thing about this dream Jenny explains further, is that there must have been a mix up at the venue, a double booking, because there are two brides. "Pity I can't remember what the other bride looked like, dreams are mad, aren't they?" Jenny finally finishes.

What makes Peter remember this dream in particular is what happens after breakfast. Even though the morning is bright and sunny, it's still early and there's a light dusting of frost coating all the garden surfaces. As he's about to make a run to the recycling bin in his pyjamas, he retreats back to the kitchen when he feels a blast of cold air as he opens the back door. Spotting Jenny's cosy pink dressing gown on the back of the kitchen chair, he pulls it around himself for his dash outside.

It's taking a bit of force to lift the lid on the blue recycling bin, the frost had made it a little resistant to being opened. There's a small popping sound as the lid finally separates from the bin. Peter spots some small movement from the corner of his eye and notices a little robin redbreast watching him intently from his perch on top of the black refuse bin that sits next to the recycling one. Thinking it strange that the bird hasn't moved or even flinched given his proximity and the noise he's making, Peter returns it stare.

Forgetting the coldness of the morning, Peter is momentarily transfixed and locking eyes with the small bird, he has convinced himself there's something special about this bird. Maybe Jenny is right when she insists the robin is the spirit of a loved come back to check in. Peter could swear that bird was winking at him and from what he could make out it was holding something dark green in its mouth.

Jenny is wondering where her dressing gown is gone when she returns from hallway, after turning up the heat on the thermostat, and is met with an excited Peter, telling her in a hurried tone that he has just met her late mother. Jenny is flabbergasted by this and follows a flustered Peter out to the bins, even though she's still in her pyjamas, she doesn't notice the cold as she runs after him. As she turns the corner to the small area where the bins are kept, a disappointed Peter tells her it's too late—she's gone. All that's left to show for Peter's encounter is a small piece of dark green seaweed sitting atop the bin lid that had been in the bird's beak a few seconds earlier. The seaweed made sense to Jenny as her mother always loved the sea and maybe this is what had convinced Peter too of her identity.

Returning back to the warmth of the kitchen, Jenny is surprised by Peter's reaction to the bird, he had always poured scorn on her superstitious beliefs. A visit from her late mother in the form of a robin didn't surprise her as much as Peter's change of heart.

"To think, the first time I get to meet your mother, I'm wearing a pink fluffy dressing gown!" Peter is laughing now as Jenny assures him, "That colour suits you much better than me."

Epilogue
14th February 2023
Back to Normal

It came as a surprise to Emma, herself, that in a weird way she missed Paul. It wasn't that they had been close to each other in recent years. They did have a bond though; each knew the other's dark secrets and Paul Lombard was the only person Emma felt was on her level. He just got her.

Never being one for sentimentality, Emma didn't ever visit his grave, but in her own way did memorialise him. In her second book, she painted him in a much more flattering light and made him the main character, an anti-hero that does things his own way. Aesthetically, she had described him as his younger self, and has based the physical characteristics on Paul when she was going out with him. They would have both been in their early twenties then and Paul was very good looking, the trouble was he knew it.

Emma didn't waste any time on regret and hasn't given the photograph of Gull Cove that she sent to Paul's phone a second thought. The photo had been sent as a timely reminder to Paul to keep his mouth shut about covering up for her murdering that old priest, as she knew he had helped Penny